I'M OFF
TO MONTANA
FOR TO
THROW
THE HOOLIHAN

CODE OF THE WEST

BOOK SIX

I'M OFF TO MONTANA FOR TO THROW THE HOOLIHAN

Stephen Bly

CROSSWAY BOOKS • WHEATON, ILLINOIS

A DIVISION OF GOOD NEWS PUBLISHERS

I'm Off to Montana for to Throw the Hoolihan

Published by Crossway Books
      a division of Good News Publishers
      1300 Crescent Street
      Wheaton, Illinois 60187

Cover illustration: George Bush

First printing 1997

Printed in the United States of America

Library of Congress Cataloging-in-Publication Data
Bly, Stephen A., 1944-
    I'm off to Montana for to throw the hoolihan / Stephen Bly.
       p.   cm.—(Code of the West; bk. 6)
    ISBN 0-89107-953-X
    I. Title II. Series: Bly, Stephen A., 1944- Code of the West :
    bk. 6.
    PS3552.L93I47   1997
    813'.54—dc21   97-17736

07	06	05	04	03	02	01	00	99	98	97
15	14	13	12	11	10	9	8	7	6	5	4	3	2	1

For
STEPHEN ARTHUR WALSTON
"Little Hoolie"

1

onday, October 1, 1883, Bull Mountain Ferry, Yellowstone River, Montana Territory.

M "That little woman of yours looks about ready to start calvin' any day now!" The speaker had two missing upper front teeth, a month-old red beard, plus a shirt so dirty it was impossible to determine where the material ended and the dirt and grease began. Even a cool autumn breeze drifting down the middle of the Yellowstone River couldn't diminish his odor. "I reckon I've seen some big'ns before, but that one will come out walkin' and talkin'."

Pepper Andrews, still sitting in the wagon, didn't bother to sit up straight and suck her stomach in. But she did turn to her husband and speak in a rather loud and slightly husky voice. "Tap, would you please hand me up a gun? I believe I need to kill this foul-smelling, disgusting excuse for a man who just insulted me."

The ferryman scooted back from the wagon toward the steam-driven donkey engine that propelled the craft. "What'd she say?" he rasped.

Angelita poked her eleven-year-old brown face out from under a wool blanket next to Pepper. "She said she was going to kill you. Can I watch?"

"No, you most certainly can't!" Pepper replied, flopping the blanket back over Angelita's head. "Mr. Andrews, may I see your revolver?"

"She's joshin' me, ain't she?" the flushed man choked.

Tap wiped his thick dark brown mustache with his hand and pushed his black beaver felt hat to the back of his head, his brown eyes as uncommitted as a riverboat gambler's. "Mrs. Andrews has been a bit touchy lately when someone mentions her, eh, her physique."

"Do I get the revolver?" Pepper demanded. "Or do I have to use the shotgun under the seat?"

"Look, folks, this has gone far enough," the man pleaded. "I was jist tryin' to be friendly. Idle conversation, that's all it was."

"Don't use the shotgun, dear," Tap urged. "At this range it would . . . splatter."

A muffled voice of a curious girl filtered up from the blanket. "Why can't I watch this time?"

The ferryman took another step back and balanced himself on the far rail of the platform ferry. The roar and hiss of the steam engine almost drowned his shout. "This time? What kind of woman are you married to? You mean she's done this before?"

Tap pulled his .44 Colt out of his holster. Holding it by the barrel, he started to hand it up to Pepper and then brought it back down. "Do you have to kill him? Couldn't you just maim him? Maybe shoot him in the legs or something?"

"No. I've thought it through. I believe I'll kill him." Pepper ran her fingers through soiled blonde hair, brushing it back between her hat and the collar of her coat. She had given up ten days earlier trying to keep it pinned up in her combs. The gold dangling earrings that grazed against her hand felt cold, but her neck was very warm.

Tap started to hand the gun back up to her. "Well, you have to promise me you won't gut-shoot him. I don't want this poor man to be in agony for two or three days before he dies."

Pepper glanced over at the cowering man.

"This ain't funny!" the ferryman protested.

"All right," she said, "I won't gut-shoot him."

Tap shrugged. "Sorry, partner, that's the best I could do for you. Hope you're settled up with the Almighty. At least you won't be gut-shot."

"You're givin' her your pistol?" he wailed. "She's actin' crazy!

A woman like that shouldn't be allowed to have a gun. Someone could get hurt by accident!"

"Oh, it won't be by accident. A man's got to keep the wife happy. You married?"

"Eh . . . no."

"Just as well, seeing how things are turning out. I can notify your next of kin if you'd like."

"You ain't goin' to let her shoot an unarmed man!" he pleaded as Tap handed her the gun.

He could see the man eyeing the river as if considering a hasty and wet retreat. "Well, there is one thing you could try," Tap drawled, dragging out each word.

The man's voice cracked. "What's that?"

"You could apologize for hintin' that she was a little overweight. You could, perhaps, say what a fine-lookin', thin woman she is . . . but that's up to you, mister." He glanced up at Pepper. "Now, darlin', try to take care of things with just one bullet. There's no use wastin' valuable ammunition."

"Wait!" the ferryman hollered. "Ma'am, you surely are . . . eh, one of the finest-lookin' ladies I ever did see. Yes, ma'am . . . you are as purdy as one of them actresses in Cheyenne."

"And thin?" she questioned, dangling the revolver in her right hand.

"Oh yes, ma'am, very thin indeed—a picture of feminine loveliness!"

Pepper adjusted the hat ribbon around her chin. "Did you hear that, Tap?"

He nodded and smiled.

"I heard it," came Angelita's muffled reply.

"Thank you, sir. This gentleman is obviously very perceptive and has a trained eye for beautiful women." Pepper lifted her nose in the air and tried for a fresh breath.

The ferryman released a long, deep sigh and returned to his steam engine. Several times he glanced over his shoulder at Tap and Pepper.

Pepper eyed the approaching shoreline and patted the worn wooden seat for Tap to climb up and join her. As he swung up,

she shoved the .44 back into his holster. He untied the reins from
the hand brake.

"Can I come out now?" Angelita asked.

"Come on up, girl," Tap laughed. "We'll be at the house before
dark . . . providin' someone don't rile Mama again."

The sky was gray with thin, wispy clouds that hinted of winter's coming. But they showed no threat of immediate precipita-
tion. The buckboard, piled high with belongings, rattled its way
north over the parallel tracks in the treeless prairie. Thick
bunches of brown grass and scattered sage filled the landscape
from the Yellowstone River up the gradual grade to the Bull
Mountains.

The wooden hubs of the wagon wheels creaked. The buckboard springs bounced. The hooves of the draft horses clopped
ahead of them. Onespot and Roundhouse, the saddle horses tethered behind the wagon, whinnied.

The air was dry and slightly cool, but Pepper felt sweat form
on the back of her neck and forehead. Her back ached. Her der-
riere seemed permanently attached to the wagon seat. The beginning of the two-week journey north from Pine Bluffs was a dim
picture in her memory. She could not remember a time when she
wasn't pregnant. The plain, long brown dress was the only one she
owned that she could still wear. She refused to alter or purchase
another.

I will burn this the day the baby is born!

Lord, why couldn't anything have been average?

I knew I was going to get big—but not this big.

I knew I would grow weary—but not this tired.

I knew it would seem like a very long time—but not for eternity.

*It's time to get this over with. I'm ready. The baby's ready. He's
been kicking and slugging me for months. If we get to the house
tonight, I'm going to lay down in bed and not get up until that
baby's born.*

Frankly, Lord, with all Your wisdom and power, couldn't You could have figured out a better system than this? At least a more comfortable one?

Pepper slipped her gloved hand through Tap's right arm. The stiff canvas jacket felt rough as she leaned against it. He patted the top of her hand. His brown eyes were lost in thought on the northern horizon. She laid her face against his sleeve.

But he has his ranch.

Our ranch.

Thanks to Stack.

The Lowrey and Andrews Land and Cattle Co.

When this baby's born, we'll all forget these last lousy nine months. It's been tough on him too. He worries about my health. It's always on his mind. I can read it in his eyes.

Like right now.

I wish he wouldn't worry about me so much.

She snuggled up a little closer.

Tap glanced down at Pepper clutching his arm. Then he slapped the reins. The horses picked up their pace.

"Come on, Gringo! Come on, TwoShoes! Heyaah!"

I ought to be able to run 600 pairs of cows and calves down here most all summer. There's plenty of water. The grass looks thick. I'll take the steers up to the hills. . . . 'Course, I'll need to put on some cowpunchers for the summer. I think I can winter out with just four men—hire a crew for the roundups and maybe keep on six, eight men all summer. Lorenzo's a good man. I wish I had Wiley, but it's not right to ask him to leave his place down in Texas.

The 500 head we bought from Tom Slaughter will give us some increase in the spring. Then we'll buy 2,000 head of Texas beef cows, but that depends on how we scout it out. Stack wasn't sure of the boundaries. I'll go into Billings and check out the county maps. Maybe we'll spend the winter puttin' boundary markers out. . . . Probably spend the winter choppin' firewood and keepin' the place warm for Lil' Tap.

Out of the corner of his eye, Tap glanced down at Pepper's ample stomach.

Lord, I surely hope I know what I'm doin' bein' a daddy. I don't even have this husband stuff down very good yet. My only confidence is that others have gone on before and somehow survived.

I reckon we will too.

Right, Lord?

He glanced back over his shoulder at the Yellowstone River. The ferryboat steamed back across. He could hear the distant blast of its whistle.

"That old boy at the ferry will have quite a story to tell 'em at the saloon tonight." He grinned. "You came across mighty serious, darlin'."

Pepper sat up and tried to stretch her back. Giving up on any relief, she folded her hands across the stomach that filled her lap like a lunch basket. A full, immense, overflowing lunch basket. "I was serious."

Angelita swatted a giant mosquito off her brown cheek and wrinkled her nose. "How come you made me hide under the blanket?" she asked. "I've seen men get shot before."

"Because," Tap reached around Pepper and tousled Angelita's black bangs, "we just wanted to scare the man. Having you hide made it seem more realistic. Pepper wasn't really goin' to shoot him."

"I seriously thought about it!" Pepper insisted. "The next person that even hints about me being fat is dead. This is all your fault, Tapadera Andrews!" She pointed to her protruding stomach.

"My fault? It's, eh, it's not all my fault."

"Sure it is," she argued. "If you had never pretended that you were Hatcher and never come up to Colorado to claim that ranch . . . why, then this would never have happened."

"You'd be in some dance hall, and I'd be back on the border dodgin' lawmen. Sounds pretty boring to me." He winked and then gave her a squeeze. "I'm mighty glad it turned out this way, Mrs. Aimee Pepper Paige Andrews!"

Pepper pulled his head closer and kissed the stubble of a three-day beard that clung to the side of Tap's tanned face.

"You're not supposed to do that!" Angelita broke in.

"Do what?" Pepper asked.

"That kissing stuff."

"Why not?"

"A woman great with child is not supposed to kiss."

"Says who?" Tap demanded.

"I read it in a book."

"What kind of books are you reading?"

"It was in the library."

"Well, it was wrong," Tap continued. "You aren't supposed to ride buckin' horses when you're in a motherly condition, but it's all right to kiss your husband." Tap leaned down and kissed Pepper on the lips.

"If you two are going to keep that up, I'm going back under the blanket."

"We'll try to control ourselves," Pepper assured her.

"Well, I should hope so!" Angelita pulled her long black pigtails around to the front of her dress and began to twirl one in each hand. "That reminds me. I've been wondering, what do a husband and a wife do on their honeymoon?"

Pepper coughed and tried to clear her throat.

Tap stared up the road. "I've got to drive the team, Pepper, darlin'. Why don't you answer Angelita's question?"

Pepper took a deep breath. "Exactly why did you ask that question?"

"Well, Daddy and Mrs. Baker got married, and she left her five kids with a sister of hers in Denver. Then she and Daddy were going to go down to Colorado Springs for a honeymoon. But Daddy can't move his left arm much, and his legs are next to useless. They can't go for a walk or swing in the park or shop. What do you think they're doing?"

"With five children of her own, she probably just likes sitting still on a bench and holding hands."

"That sounds pretty boring."

Tap glanced back over his shoulder. "We got some riders coming up behind us. Looks like some drovers."

"Do you think they kissed?"

"Who? Those drovers?" Tap teased.

"No!" Angelita huffed. "My daddy and Mrs. Baker. Do you think they kissed on their honeymoon?"

"Mrs. Baker? Are you just going to call her Mrs. Baker?" Pepper quizzed.

"At least when I'm not around them. She might be married to my daddy, but she's not my mother, and you didn't answer my question."

"About them kissing?"

"Yeah. Do you really think they did?"

"Yes," Pepper replied, "I think they probably kissed. What do you think, Mr. Andrews?"

Tap glanced over his shoulder again. The riders were gaining ground behind them. "I think . . . Angelita, grab that shotgun off the floor and hold it under your blanket."

"Trouble?" Pepper asked.

"Just cautious." Tap pulled his '73 Winchester rifle from the scabbard in the back of the wagon, cocked it, and laid it across his lap. He drove the team to the right of the roadway and slowed to a walk, giving the drovers room to ride around him.

Instead, three of them pulled up alongside the parked wagon. The fourth rider hung back near Onespot and Roundhouse who were tied to the rear of the wagon. A man with bushy gray sideburns dropped his reins on his black horse's neck. He leaned with both hands on the narrow rawhide-wrapped saddle horn. "Howdy, folks. Looks like you all are movin'."

Tap's right hand rested on the receiver of his rifle. "Yep."

"You movin' in or out of this country?"

"We're moving in," Pepper announced.

Tap studied the eyes of each man. He figured at least two had been drinking. They were the ones ready to make a play for their guns. "I reckon you boys are headed back to the ranch. What outfit you ride for?"

"Where we work ain't none of your business, mister." The clean-shaven spokesman stared at Pepper. "You folks must have made a wrong turn at the river. There ain't no farmin' land up this way."

"We didn't make any mistake. We've got a place up the trail a piece," Tap insisted.

The oldest of the four men looked about forty. He spat a wad of tobacco juice over the top of his chestnut horse's head, then turned to Tap, his hand on the grip of his holstered .45. "Maybe you farmers don't understand. We don't want you up in this country. There ain't no farmland available. You come up here and try to stake a claim on ranch country, you'll get yourself hurt. We're just tryin' to help you. So turn the wagon around and mosey on up the river. Maybe there's some farmland left down there near Billings."

"This here gray gelding is a fine-lookin' horse," the fourth man called out. "Ain't no farm horse. I'll buy him from you for ten cash dollars, mister."

"The horses aren't for sale." Tap's brown eyes met Angelita's dark brown ones. He nodded slightly toward the back of the wagon.

"Maybe you didn't hear me," the man at the rear of the wagon began. "I said I was goin' to—"

"Angelita," Tap interrupted in a loud, commanding voice, "if he touches either horse of mine, aim that Greener at his belly and pull the trigger."

She stood up. The blanket dropped, and she pointed the shotgun at the man. The man with the bushy gray sideburns went for his revolver, but Tap's cocked rifle slammed into the man's wrist and rested in his ribs.

"I hope you don't think for a minute that she won't pull the trigger. And I can shoot you at this range even if I'm dead!" Tap growled. "You boys want to have it out, let's do it right now. Mister, you and your horse-stealin' buddy in the back are dead the minute the first shot is fired. So what's it going to be?"

Tap hadn't noticed that Pepper had pulled his revolver. She now pointed it at the clean-shaven man wearing wide suspenders. "Actually, I believe three of them are dead. Gentlemen, I do not intend to lose my baby's father."

"You caught us on a bad day, boys. We're tired, sore, and a little short of patience. We just don't feel like playin' games. So if you'd like to go down in history as the gang wiped out by a man in a wagon, a woman about to go into labor, and a kid with a shotgun, be my guest!" Tap challenged.

"Whoa! Folks, we ain't talkin' about shootin' anyone. No, sir," sideburns explained.

Tap checked back at Pepper and Angelita.

"Oh, really?" Pepper let the hammer down slowly on Tap's .44 and forced a smile.

"Oh, yeah . . . we wasn't goin' to shoot you or nothin'! Why, no, ma'am. Jist figured on scarin' you out like the others."

"Well, isn't that nice, dear? They aren't goin' to kill us after all." Tap raised the rifle until it was aimed at the man's neck. "Boys, you're liquored up and actin' crazy. Now ride on up ahead of us, and remember this rifle and peep sight are good to at least 600 yards. You turn back or fire a shot, and I'll drop you dead on the prairie quicker than you can say, 'Texas fever.' I don't have much patience with men who go around threatenin' women and children, so don't push me."

"Look, mister, you're gettin' in over your head. You don't know who you're dealin' with," one man growled.

"Tap," Pepper sighed, "I'm tired . . . really tired. Let's just shoot 'em all now and go on to the ranch."

"Tap!" the older man exclaimed. "You ain't that there Tapadera Andrews, are you?"

Tap's rifle was now aimed at the man's head.

The thin, dark-skinned man cleared his throat. "You the one that cleaned out Cabe and Banner down in Wyomin'?"

"Yeah, that was me and Odessa. I suppose you're going to tell me you're a relative of theirs?"

"Shoot, no," the man replied. "Cabe cheated me at cards once in El Paso, and we ended up in a knife fight. Relax, boys. This here is none other than Tap Andrews. I'm called Tennessee."

"I'm Donnie-Bill," the rear rider introduced himself. "I heard you stopped fifty men at the depot in Cheyenne City."

"Me and Pepper and Angelita stopped 'em. But there weren't fifty."

"Did she say you were goin' to a ranch?" Tennessee asked.

"Yeah, me and a friend are taking over the Slash-Bar-4."

"You don't say! We're stayin'—I mean, workin' the Pothook-H just a little bit north of your range. We owe you all an apology. We had no business harassin' our new neighbors, did we, Cow Town?"

"No, sir," the clean-shaven man in the soiled black coat replied. "We been into . . . eh, Miles City on a tear and ain't thinkin' real good. Now we're headed back to the ranch. Probably won't get back down to town until spring."

"We figured you for some more farmers," Tennessee admitted.

"More farmers?" Tap asked.

"Oh, some Quakers moved in at Badger Canyon. That's up past your place. But don't you worry about them none. Their crops mysteriously burned up a couple weeks ago, didn't they, boys? We figure they won't last the winter."

"Shoot, boys, this is a great day for ranchin'!" Donnie-Bill exclaimed. "When a gunslinger the likes of Tap Andrews moves in. Yes, sir, that ought to stop any visitors from comin' up from the south."

Tap returned his rifle to his lap and took up the reins. "I didn't say I was goin' to stop any pilgrims."

"You said you was a rancher, right?"

"That's right, but I aim to get along with all my neighbors, especially the God-fearin' kind."

"Even the sodbusters?"

"As long as it's their land they're bustin'," Tap replied. "Now you boys ride on up there and keep out of our way. My wife needs some rest, and I don't plan on any more delays. Is that clear?"

"Yes, sir. Well, I'll be!" Donnie-Bill shook his head. "Tapadera Andrews ranchin' in Montana! Wait 'til I tell the others."

Their voices were starting to fade when Tap heard one mumble, "It ain't that big a deal. Ain't like the Earp boys or Stuart Brannon was moving in on the range. . . ."

Tap glanced over at Pepper, who shook her head and sighed. "Take me to my new home, Mr. Not-so-famous Gunman."

"Those four don't know beans about being drovers. Did you

notice those saddle horns have never had any ropes tied to them, let alone dallied?"

"I guess I missed that."

"They haven't been to Miles City either. It's too far away. No one could stay drunk that long, and no cowboy would have the patience to save his liquor to drink on the trail back to the ranch."

Pepper could see Tap gazing at the departing men like a marshal studying a "wanted" poster. "Tell me again about that featherbed that's waitin' for me."

"Tell us what our house is like!" Angelita pleaded.

With the four riders several hundred feet ahead of them, Tap drove the wagon onto the trail.

"We've been over all that before."

"Please!" Angelita begged.

"Well, as you two know, I was only there one night. Lorenzo and me drove those 500 head into the headquarters around noon, and I left to come get you two by sunup the next day. But as I remember, there's a nice wide veranda on all four sides, a front room about the size of our house in Pine Bluffs, and a big, long kitchen across the back. Stack has it completely furnished like some lodge for European nobility. There's a good-sized, well-stocked pantry and another fairly nice-sized room downstairs. I suppose it was the cook's room or the maid's room—something like that."

"Do I get that room? A real room all to myself?" Angelita pressed.

"Sorry, kid. You have to stay upstairs with the rest of the family." Tap winked at Angelita. "I had Stack put a big oak table in the downstairs room so I can use it for an office."

"Which upstairs bedroom do I get?" Angelita asked.

"The big one at the front is for me, Mama, and the baby," Tap reported. "You get your pick of the other three. One of 'em has a wardrobe closet big enough to corral a steer."

"All I want to know about is the featherbed." Pepper pulled her coat down over her shoulders and fanned her face with her hand. "Is it getting warmer?"

"Nope."

"You should have let me swim across the Yellowstone. That would have cooled me off."

"It wasn't nearly deep enough."

She pulled his revolver out and shoved it in his ribs without cocking the hammer. "And just what do you mean by that?"

"It wasn't deep enough for anyone to do much swimming. Don't take it personal."

"When you look as big as a chuck wagon, you take everything personal."

"Tell us about the other buildings at the headquarters," Angelita persisted.

"Again?"

"You haven't told us since last night."

"There's a barn as big as the livery in Pine Bluffs, a blacksmith's shop, a smokehouse, a bunkhouse that will accommodate a dozen men, a cook shack . . . and a cottage with a white picket fence around the backyard."

"Is that where Mr. Odessa and Miss Selena live?" Angelita asked.

"Lorenzo's there now, but Selena is staying in Billings until their weddin'." Tap let out a deep breath and shook his head. "It's hard to believe those two are gettin' married."

Pepper pulled her coat back up to her neck. "They'll make a lovely couple . . . providing they don't kill each other."

"The ranch sounds like a whole town," Angelita pondered.

"Our own little town where everything's peaceful and safe. It sounds wonderful," Pepper sighed.

"There'll be plenty of hard work for all of us," Tap cautioned.

"Mr. Andrews, if—and I do say if—I survive this pregnancy, I do believe I can survive anything," she announced.

Tap slipped his arm around her and squeezed gently. "I surely hope the rest of the kids don't give their Mama this much trouble."

"At this particular moment in history it is beyond my wildest imagination that I would ever, ever go through this again!" she informed him.

"Oh, you'll change your mind."

She took a deep breath and let it out slowly. Then she laced her gloved fingers into his callused ones. "I have a horrible, sinking feeling that you're probably right. But at the moment, I just want to go home. Let me go to sleep in a soft, clean bed, and wake me up when Lil' Tap is about six years old."

"You'll get some rest soon, Mama," Tap assured her. "We'll be there in a couple of hours."

"Rest? I'm sitting on a hardwood bench with your son doing the splits and kicking me on both sides at the same time. I just can't do anything with this child of yours."

Tap glanced over at her protruding stomach and waved his finger. "Young man, you settle down and mind your Mama right now!"

"Do babies hear anything when they're in their mommies' tummies?" Angelita asked.

"Probably not," Pepper acknowledged, "but he did stop kicking."

They rode along for several miles with very little conversation. Tap had the collar of his canvas jacket turned up. Pepper pulled her coat down again and fanned herself. Angelita kept the wool blanket over her head to ward off the cold, mosquitoes, and dust. It was the muffled, blanketed voice of Angelita that broke the silence. "I have another question."

"What's that, honey?" Pepper replied.

"Well . . . Mr. Andrews calls you Mama already."

"Yes?"

"And when little Tap or little Tapina gets big enough to talk, he'll call you Mama, right?"

"I suppose."

"Well, in order to avoid a lot of confusion . . . I was just thinking . . . maybe it would make it simpler if I just called you Mama, too."

Pepper looked over at Angelita's blanket-covered head and then at Tap. She reached up and wiped a tear from the corner of her eye. "Well, I'd be honored to have you call me Mama if that's your decision."

"We all know you aren't my mother," Angelita quickly added. "My mama's dead. But I just thought it might make things easier."

"That's mighty nice of you," Tap responded.

"Thank you," came the still-blanketed reply.

Pepper slipped her arm around Angelita and drew her close. Angelita's small brown hand reached out from under the Hudson's Bay Company wool covering and rested on Pepper's stomach.

"You know, Mr. Andrews . . . I've been waiting my entire life to have this kind of setup. When I was working the dance halls, I used to dream of this kind of life."

"Darlin', the Lord has done some wonderful things for you and me. Like savin' us, allowin' us to get married, bringin' Angelita into our family, and givin' us a friend like Stack Lowery with enough money from his gold mine to buy this ranch. You see those boulders up there at the pass?"

"Yes."

"That's the beginning of the Slash-Bar-4."

"You mean we're almost there?" Angelita squealed, emerging from her wool cocoon.

"It's quite a ways to the headquarters," Tap cautioned. "But at least the rest of the journey will be on our place."

The buildings at the Slash-Bar-4 stood on a knoll that separated the mountain grazing land from the Yellowstone River basin. From it one could see the top of the Bull Mountains in the north and almost to the river in the south.

The wide, expansive Montana sky streaked gold as the setting sun reflected off high, thin clouds. The air chilled considerably when the travelers climbed to higher ground. All three were blanket covered.

Tap startled Pepper and Angelita from their slumber. "There's some of our cows, darlin'!"

"Are we almost there?" Angelita asked.

"We should see the building just over that next knoll."

"Do the cows just hang around the barn?" Pepper asked.

"No, we'll move them down to the river range in a week or so. I told Lorenzo to keep them up here until they got the lay of the land."

The wagon rolled up the crest of the hill and began a gradual descent.

"I see it!" Angelita squealed. "Look, there it is! Is that it? That's our ranch, isn't it?"

"That's it, lil' darlin'."

"It's big—really big. Look at all those buildings! I love it! Do you love it, Mrs. Andrews—I mean, do you love it, Mama?" Angelita gulped down her final words.

"It's wonderful. Just like I imagined. Of course, at the moment any shack with a soft, clean bed would seem like heaven." Pepper stared at the ranch as Tap negotiated the wagon down the rutted lane. "Why does Lorenzo have so many cows in the corrals when there is all this grass for them to graze on?" she quizzed.

"Corrals?" Tap looked up at the headquarters. "We don't have any corrals except some little ones for horses."

"It looks like a split-rail fence all around the buildings," she insisted.

Tap stopped the wagon and stood up. "But that's just a fence to keep the cattle out of the yard. It's not—"

"I think there are cows in our front yard." Angelita pointed.

"What's goin' on? The gate must have been left open," Tap mumbled. "Where's Lorenzo?"

"That's one way to fertilize the garden." Pepper tried to stretch her arms and back. "Just get me out of this wagon!"

Tap slapped the reins on the rumps of the driving horses. Gringo and TwoShoes trotted down the slope and then up the other side of the draw toward the buildings. Tap could see at least forty or fifty head of cows wandering around the yard and buildings.

I can't believe this! I wanted everything to be perfect when we came rollin' up, and he leaves the gate down. Come on, Odessa, you're a better hand than that! I'll get Pepper tucked in the house, and then I'll mount up Roundhouse and drive them back out on the range.

They pulled through the open gate and around between the barn and the bunkhouse.

"There's a cow on the porch!" Angelita hollered.

"I can't believe this!" Tap moaned. "Where's Odessa?"

"The front door's open!" Pepper cried out.

"What?"

"There's a cow in there!" Angelita shouted.

"There can't be!" Tap fumed.

"There are cows tromping around in my home!" Pepper sobbed.

Tap drove the wagon right up to the front of the house.

"You two wait here," he ordered. "I'll check it out."

Tap reached back into the wagon, yanked out his rope, and then jumped down and sprinted up onto the porch. Slapping the indifferent, staring cow in the rump, he hollered, "Hey, yaa! Get! Get on down, cow. Hey, yaa!" The 900-pound brindle longhorn cow lumbered down the steps past the wagon and then turned back to the house and let out a loud bellow.

Tap stepped to the open front door and peered into the house. His square, broad shoulders and lanky frame almost filled the doorway. "I'd shoot you dead, but I couldn't drag you out of there!" he shouted.

"Who's in there?" Pepper called out.

Angelita jumped down from the wagon and bounded up the porch and into the house. "There's a cow in the living room . . . and another in the kitchen! There's poop everywhere!" she screamed.

"Watch out, lil' darlin', I'm goin' to chase these two out the front door. Check and see if there are any in the office!" Tap called out.

With shouts, screams, crashes, hooves hammering bare wooden floor, and hemp rope slapping on rumps, two more mottled cows lumbered out the front door, down the steps, and into the yard.

"Nothing in the office but cow manure!" Angelita reported. "I'll check upstairs."

"It's too steep. They wouldn't go up there," Tap assured her.

Angelita dashed up the wide stairway, holding her long off-white dress up to her knees, showing her black lace-up shoes.

Suddenly Tap heard a scream from upstairs. "Get out of my room!"

With broom in hand, Angelita chased a yearling calf down the stairs, across the living room, and out into the yard.

"Shoot him! Kill him! He deserves to die!" she cried out to Tap. "He pooped in my wardrobe closet!"

Tap jogged up the stairs to check out the remaining rooms and then hustled out the front door, slamming it behind him.

Pepper rocked slightly back and forth, trying to ignore the confusion around her.

"Angelita, run check the other buildings for cows," Tap hollered. He slapped a saddle on Roundhouse. "I don't want any trouble out of you," he warned the steel-gray horse. "I just don't have time."

Mounting from the right side, Tap was relieved when the horse didn't buck. Soon they were chasing the cows back out through the downed gate. Angelita caught up with him just as he pushed the last reluctant bovine out into the open pasture.

"You find any more, girl?" Tap shouted down.

"No. The bunkhouse is a bit slovenly, but all the other buildings look fine. They sure messed up the yard!"

"Can you close that gate, Angel-girl? I'll go check on Mama."

Tap rode back to the wagon and slid down off Roundhouse, draping the reins over the saddle horn. He climbed up into the wagon next to the silent Pepper.

"Well, darlin' . . . it's not like I had hoped. But . . . we're home."

Without expression or inflection she asked, "You know, it dawned on me as I sat here watching you chase cows out of our house that I have no idea in the world what it means to live out on a big cattle ranch. Does this sort of thing happen often?"

Tap thought he saw a faint sparkle in her eye. "Oh, no, ma'am. I don't reckon you'll have cows in the house more than two or three times a year."

"Oh, good," she droned. "I thought perhaps it was an everyday occurrence."

Tap grew serious. "Darlin', I don't know what to say. This should never happen, ever! I don't know what happened to Lorenzo. I don't know how that gate got left open. And I don't know who opened the front door to our house. It's a cinch those cows didn't."

Pepper started to laugh.

Just a muffled chuckle.

Then a burst of guffaws.

Finally a stampede of deep roars.

Followed by a flock of giggles.

"Darlin', are you okay?" Tap asked.

"I should have known. Why did any of this surprise me? From the day I first met you north of McCurleys' Hotel, we haven't had two ordinary, calm, peaceful, boring days in our lives!"

"You braggin' or complainin'?" he asked.

"I just want to know one thing. Is there cow dung on my featherbed?"

"Eh, no, ma'am. The bed's intact and clean, as is the bedroom itself."

"Well, sweetheart, if you and Angelita will tidy up the house, I think Lil' Tap and I will waddle up the stairs and take ourselves a nap. A very, very long nap."

2

After eleven shovelfuls of cow manure had been removed, Tap boiled water and tried to scrub up the stains. Even after the sun set, every window and shutter in the house remained flung open. A fire blazed, and vanilla boiled as they attempted to rid the place of its barnlike aroma. Both he and Angelita wore coats and gloves.

"Lil' darlin', that's about the best we can do tonight," Tap announced as they examined Angelita's upstairs room. "If you want to, you can sleep in one of the other bedrooms for the night. I don't think they smell as bad."

"It's my room—my very own room. I want to sleep here."

"I'm sorry Pepper's not awake to tuck you in tonight. I do believe she's going to sleep for a week. I'll boil some more water and unload the rest of the things in the wagon. You put away your valuables. Holler at me when you're all fixed up for bed, and I'll come up and say prayers with you."

The wagon was parked by the barn, the horses put away for the night, and the bunkhouse fairly well cleaned out. Tap sat in the drafty kitchen, still wearing coat, hat, and gloves, when Angelita scooted down the stairs. She wore her long flannel nightgown, dragging a wool blanket wrapped around her shoulders and carrying a big black comb.

"What are you doing?" She pulled a chair up next to him.

"Surmisin'."

"About what?"

"About what could have happened to Lorenzo." Tap glanced over at Angelita. "You want a cup of coffee?"

"I've told you a thousand times, coffee is not good for growing young ladies. It's not that long until my birthday."

"That's what I keep hearin'. You don't plan on gettin' married when you're twelve, do you?" he teased.

"Hah! We just move in, and you're trying to get me married off. I have a notion to stay right here until I'm thirty!"

"Well, Miss Angelita Gomez, you are hereby invited to stay with Mama and me as many years as you want to. The more, the better."

"Oh, I know that! Obviously you've grown attached to my fascinating charm and sparkling personality. It's beyond your comprehension to think of me being anywhere but here."

Tap snickered and then sighed. "Well, I wouldn't have used those exact words, but I catch the drift. How do you come up with phrases like that?"

"Did I say it wrong?"

"How would I know?"

Angelita wrinkled her nose as she pulled a heavy comb through her waist-length black hair. "You know, I'm really, really glad to be here, even if it does smell bad. And I'm very happy that you and Mrs. Andrews—you and Mama let me stay with you."

"We both feel mighty fortunate to have you with us."

"It was the Lord's leading, you know."

"You're right about that."

Angelita glanced at the coffee on the stove. "I wish I had some hot milk. When are we going to get a milk cow?"

"I plan on buyin' one after the weddin'. 'Course we've got to find the groom before we can have a weddin'."

"Maybe he went to see Miss Selena."

"That could be. But it doesn't really add up. Maybe it will seem clearer in the mornin'. That's what I've been sittin' here tryin' to figure out. Lorenzo's a good man. He wouldn't leave the headquarters knowin' I was due any day now unless it was an emergency."

"What kind of emergency?"

Tap pulled his gloves off and wrapped his fingers around the steaming tin coffee cup. "Only two I can think of . . . either something here on the ranch, like wolves killin' the cattle. In which case he'll probably come draggin' in late tonight."

"What's the other?"

"Selena. If she sent word for him to come a runnin', I reckon he would."

"But wouldn't he leave a note or something?"

"That's one of the things that bothers me."

"What else bothers you?"

"That yard gate being open and the door to the house left open. Lorenzo wouldn't do that no matter what the emergency. It don't figure."

"You mean, 'it doesn't figure.' The correct word is *doesn't*."

Tap grinned. "Nothin' like havin' two women in the house to nag at me."

"Your progress is slow even then."

"Come on, Angel-girl, I'm goin' to tuck you in."

They crossed through the front room and hiked up the stairs hand in hand. "You going to sleep in that big featherbed with Mama?" she asked him.

"Not tonight. I don't want to take a chance of wakin' her up. In fact, you and me better figure on cookin' meals tomorrow. Mama and Lil' Tap are mighty bushed after that long trip up from Pine Bluffs."

"Why do you always call the baby Lil' Tap? Do you like boys better than girls?"

"I guess I call him Lil' Tap because I've already got a fascinating and charming daughter." He leaned down and gave her a squeeze.

"Yes." Her eyes widened with a satisfied sparkle. "I can certainly see your point."

"Now come on, you. Let's thank the good Lord and get you snuggled under them covers."

"*Those* covers," Angelita corrected with a musical jingle in her voice.

Around midnight Tap eased off the leather sofa, closed all the windows, and stoked the fire. He lit a kerosene lantern and hiked out to the bunkhouse and then over to the barn to see if Lorenzo Odessa had returned.

He hadn't.

Tap was up boiling coffee by 4:00 A.M. He had Roundhouse saddled and ready to ride by daybreak. Holding his spurs in one hand and his hat in the other, he crept quietly up the stairs to Pepper's room.

For several moments he studied her face, the only part of her not covered by the mountain of blankets.

"Well, Mama," he sighed, "you are a purdy lady even when you're ready to deliver."

"I bet you say that to all the girls!" she replied without opening her eyes.

"I didn't know you were awake."

"Yes, I've been awake all night waiting for my husband to come to bed."

"No foolin'?"

"Well, actually I just woke up. This is undoubtedly the most comfortable bed in the entire world."

"Darlin', I'm going to ride out to look for Lorenzo."

"You think he's in trouble?"

"I don't know what to think. He's not the type to get drunk and forget to come home. Angelita will stir up some breakfast for you and help you get out to the privy and all."

"I might be as big as a smokehouse, but I can still stroll out to the privy on my own. How does our house smell this morning?"

"Either it smells a little better, or I'm gettin' used to it."

"When will you be back?"

"Around noon."

"You promise?"

"Yep. And do you promise not to have that baby while I'm gone?"

"Dr. Haffner said not 'til the first of November."

"Doctors have been wrong."

"Let's hope so. If your son grows any bigger in there, you'll have to buy him a horse instead of a pony."

Tap leaned over the bed and kissed her slightly chapped lips. "Bye, darlin'."

"I love you, Mr. Andrews."

"And I love both of you!"

Roundhouse bucked twice as they left the yard and a couple more times when Tap stopped to close the yard gate. After that the gray gelding decided to settle down and allow Tap to take charge. The thin clouds of the previous day had disappeared and left a faint blue autumn sky. It wasn't freezing, but the cool air carried a hint that frosty weather wasn't too far away.

This was Tap's third trip to the Slash-Bar-4. A month earlier he and Stack Lowery had spent three days on a quick ride around. Then he and Lorenzo had brought up the 500 head of cattle from Pine Bluffs, but Tap had only stayed the night.

Most of the 50,000-acre ranch remained unexplored. Tap knew that someday he would know every creek, dry wash, draw, and coulee. He knew that the day would come when the boulders, sage, and chaparral would read like a familiar map. He knew that in years to come, he would be able to drop the reins on Roundhouse's neck and tell him to head to the barn, then go to sleep in the saddle, and wake up at home.

All of that would happen someday.

But Tap was well aware that this was not that day.

For both horse and rider it was unfamiliar territory.

If Lorenzo's in trouble out there, it could take a week to find him. If he was on foot, he'd build a signal fire or something. 'Course a lot of this ranch doesn't have anything to burn. If he just lost his mount, he'd walk back to the ranch in half a day or so. If he got shot . . . well, if he got shot, he's dead by now.

Four miles east of the headquarters, he cut across the trail of an unshod horse heading south toward the river. "Looks as if some Crow took a shortcut across the ranch to hunt up in the mountains. But I don't know why he couldn't hunt on his side of the river."

He stood in his tapadera-covered stirrups and stared down

toward the river. The dry grass and sage were no more than a foot tall for miles.

"Well, partner," he drawled to Roundhouse, "there's no ponies between us and the Yellowstone. The one that came by here must be back on the reservation. Sort of makes me curious about what he was huntin' up there—pronghorns . . . or longhorns?"

Tap followed the Indian's tracks for several miles up into the Bull Mountains. He was surprised to find that a couple dozen head of Slash-Bar-4 cattle had grazed that far from the headquarters. Working the brush, Tap herded them up and pushed them back down into the open prairie.

"You girls go on home!" he shouted. "I don't know how you got up here without being driven. Go on! Heyaah! You stay out in the open, and I'll pick you up on the way back."

If someone was drivin' off our cows already, then maybe Lorenzo did ride up here. But I don't think one Indian would drive off a dozen head.

At the base of a limestone bluff, Tap spotted the remnants of a campfire. He slipped down out of the saddle for an inspection.

It's a day or two old. Indian fire. He carried an antelope over to the rock and dressed him out. The coyotes finished off ever'thin' but the hooves. This is ranch land, but as long as they don't start butcherin' beef, there's not much for me to say. Maybe Lorenzo came upon him sudden like and . . . but I don't see any shoed horseprints.

Tap circled the limestone bluff and tried to find Lorenzo's sign. But the only prints he saw were from the Indian.

"Well, Roundhouse, I told Mama we'd be back by noon. Could be that Lorenzo is home by now anyway. Let's ride up to those cedars on the mesa, then cut back, pick up the cows, and go home. We might not make it by 12:00, but we'll be out on the slope where she can see us if she's worried."

The mesa was mostly grass and sage, with scrub cedars spread wide apart. Tap stood in the stirrups and surveyed the area. There was nothing but more hills and mountains to the north and sloping prairie to the south. He was ready to turn back toward the headquarters when he spotted two blackbirds diving at and harassing a raven.

"You like dead meat, big boy. Just exactly where is your dinner that those blackbirds don't want you to have?"

The raven dipped in the sky toward a cluster of ten-foot cedars and then fled the attack of the birds one-fourth its size. Tap rode straight to the cedars and caught a whiff of the dead horse before he reached the carcass.

That's Lorenzo's horse . . . at least what's left of it. Shot in the neck. He's been threatenin' to shoot it. But you don't shoot your own horse in the neck. Maybe between the eyes if you have to put him down. But not in the neck. No saddle . . . no brass casings where Lorenzo fired back. Nothing.

Tap rode in an increasingly wider circle around the dead animal until he cut a trail going north. *Draft horses? Someone's ridin' some big boys out here. They snuck up and shot Lorenzo's horse while ridin' draft horses?*

He spent the next hour searching the mesa for any trace of Lorenzo Odessa. Then he turned back to the large prints of the draft animals. He followed them into the mountains. Tap reined up suddenly and glanced back down the slope.

I told Pepper I'd be home around noon. She'll be worried. But . . . Lorenzo's on foot. I don't reckon he's dead, or I'd have found the body. Maybe he's hikin' back to the ranch. Either that or he rode off on the draft horse. Rode off where? Where are these tracks leadin'? She'll understand. A man's got to look after his friends.

Tap rode Roundhouse three steps and then turned around.

And a man's got to take care of his family. What if she's hurtin'? What if it's her time? Lord, this isn't a good bind to be in either way.

Tap caught himself rubbing the back of his neck and staring down at the saddle horn. "Come on, Andrews, you've got to do one or the other."

Finally he spurred Roundhouse back down the slope of the mountains toward where he had driven the cattle.

"Lorenzo," Tap lectured to the wind, "if you're dead, I can't help you much. If you're alive, you went off with those draft horses, and I assume you can hang on until I catch up. And if you're hikin' home, I surely hope you're out on the slope so I can spot you."

By midafternoon he turned the cows out and rode up to the headquarters. Angelita met him at the gate.

"You're late," she called out.

"You could see me comin' in, couldn't you?"

"Yes." Angelita, wrapped in coat and knit hat, opened the gate, waited for Tap to ride into the yard, and then closed it. "Did you find Mr. Odessa?"

"Not exactly."

"What do you mean?"

Tap leaned down and lifted Angelita up on the horse behind him. "Come on, let's go see Mama so I only have to tell this story once."

Angelita washed the supper dishes while Pepper lounged on a pillow-lined wooden chair beside the table. Tap stuffed some biscuits and a small tin of ground coffee into an empty flour sack.

"You should have kept on Lorenzo's trail. But I'm really glad you came back," Pepper admitted.

"Darlin', I don't like breakin' promises to you. Besides, I didn't have a bedroll or grub bag. I had hopes he'd be hoofin' it back this way."

"You think you'll be gone more than one night?" Pepper asked.

"If I leave at daybreak, I can get to the mesa before noon. The best I figure is catching up with them by tomorrow night. Even if ever'thing's all right, I can't be back before two, maybe three days. This is a big ranch. Are you two going to be okay here?"

She spoke softly. "I think so."

"The cows can take care of themselves, and Angelita can feed the horses. I'm taking Lorenzo's roan horse for him to ride back on."

"Are you sure he'll be in any condition to ride?"

"Well . . ." Tap paused and looked toward the front door. "I'm bringin' him home one way or another. But I'm countin' on him bein' all right. I never heard of killers ridin' big old draft horses."

Pepper began to giggle.

"What's the matter?" Tap quizzed. "You sure been laughin' a lot lately."

"Either laughing or crying."

"So what is it this time?" he pressed.

"I believe one of the reasons we moved to Montana was to get a fresh start in a quiet and peaceful place," she snickered. "We didn't even get ten minutes of peace."

Tap admired her green eyes. "Well, it's quiet out here."

"And I have a very comfortable bed."

"And a house that smells like a stall," Tap reminded her.

"It's getting better. Besides, me and the Lord talked that all out this morning."

"Oh? What did He say?"

"He said that if it was good enough for the baby Jesus, it's good enough for Lil' Tap."

"Can't argue with Him on that, can we? I'll pull out early and let you two sleep. I promise to be back within two or three days or send word as to what's going on. And I do keep my promises."

Pepper reached her hand out and pulled him close. "I know it, cowboy. That's what keeps me sane."

The clouds were hanging low and heavy by the time Tap reached the remains of Lorenzo's horse the next day. He figured it was before noon but couldn't gauge by the sun. Circling the carcass a couple of times, he spied the prints of the big draft horses and followed the trail northward.

The trees never got very thick or tall where he crested the hills and descended into a small valley. He walked the horses down the grade, allowing them to stop and graze wherever there were a few clumps of grass. The huge prints were easy to follow, although the weight of the animals made it impossible to guess whether either one carried more than one rider.

He remounted and continued the ride. Where the trees began to thin, a steep, walled canyon stretched to the north. He came to the stream, and the draft horse tracks turned north toward the distant canyon. Daylight faded as evening came on. The heavy clouds lost some of their moisture. It was more like a cold mist—a heavy, wet, dripping fog—than a rain.

Lord, a good rain could take this track out. That would mean ridin' up this little valley for nothin'. But no one's going to straddle a draft horse for more than a day. It would bust 'em in two. There's got to be a camp or a shack or somethin' in that canyon.

The drizzling rain let up about dark. Tap stopped near the still-dry creekbed and made a fire, hovering over it like a chuck-wagon cook until he finally dried out a little. He broke a pine knot out of a decaying log. Once he had the pitch blazing, he grabbed it by the stem, kicked out his fire, and led the two horses along as he followed the draft horse trail by torchlight.

Although he couldn't see more than five feet in front of him, Tap could tell that the brushy valley had opened up to a meadow south of the canyon entrance. It looked fairly level, wide, and totally black.

"It's gettin' so dark I can't tell what we're ridin' through," he mumbled at the slowly plodding horses. "Maybe it's time to call it a night."

Tap tied Roundhouse and Peanut to a bull pine and hiked down near the creekbed. The pine knot had been reduced to a bright red glow. Jamming the handle into a crevice between two large rocks, he left it and groped his way into the brush, feeling for firewood.

This is mighty wet, but maybe it will puff up and make a flame. Providin' that ember lasts a little longer.

It didn't.

A rifle shot shattered the pine knot, throwing sparks for several feet. Six more shots followed.

Two pistols and a carbine most likely. Maybe three pistols.

Lying flat on the rocks near the creekbed, Tap clutched his Colt .44. He dragged himself through mud puddles and jagged boulders toward what he hoped was the horses. In the distance he heard the shouts of several men.

Reaching Roundhouse, Tap pulled his '73 Winchester from the scabbard and slowly checked the lever. Hunkered in the mud, he leaned against the trunk of a tree and pointed the rifle in the general direction of the voices.

Come on, boys, show your hand. You do want to know if you had any success, don't ya?

"Did you get him, Cow Town?"

Cow Town? Are these the same bunch as on the trail yesterday? Since when do cowhands start bushwhackin' strangers?

"I musta. He ain't shootin' back. I blew that torch right out of his hands. Did you see that shot?"

"We all leaded him down pretty good. He's got more holes than an old maid's weddin' dress."

"Didn't take us long to eliminate that gunslinger."

"He ain't much."

"We ought to just blast that farmer."

"Boss says we have to drive 'em out alive."

"The boss ain't here."

"Well, we cain't leave this one up here, or someone will come lookin' for him. Let's pack his body down to the river. They'll blame it on the Indians."

"Light yourself a torch, Tennessee. Go see if he's dead."

"I ain't lightin' no torch and gettin' myself shot, no sir."

"But you said you nailed him."

"Maybe he's only mostly nailed. What if he has the strength to pull the trigger? You go check him out."

"You boys are about as brave as the ladies' missionary society."

"We ain't stupid."

"And I ain't goin' to sit here sprawled in the brush until mornin'."

"Okay, here goes," one of them shouted. "I'll jist hold this here torch in my hand."

Mister, you aren't goin' to be within five feet of that light.

A sulfur match flared up. Some twigs began to burn about fifty yards straight in front of Tap. He didn't shoot but aimed the rifle about five feet to the left of the flames. *Make your move, boys.*

"I say he either hightailed it out of the country, or he's laying there dead."

"Let's find his horses. We ought to make somethin' out of this."

"Spread out. We won't find a thing all bunched up."

Tap could hear boot heels breaking sticks, coming toward the horses. He waited near Roundhouse.

"I think them horses is over here, boys!" the man hollered.

A match flickered near Roundhouse's rump, all that separated Tap from the gunman. Andrews jabbed the gray horse in the ribs with the butt of his rifle. His head tied to a tree, the big gelding whinnied and threw a hind-legged kick. The match flicked to the mud and died as one hoof caught the man in the pit of the stomach. The other crashed into his shoulder. He tumbled backwards, and it was once again dark.

"Tennessee? What happened? Where's them horses?" a voice to the right shouted. "Tennessee?"

"That horse coldcocked him with a kick. I seen it from here! You cain't sneak up on a horse in the dark."

"Grab a torch and let's find them horses. If that ol' boy ain't shot at us by now, he's dead."

Another match flared up. This time the man held the flickering light far away from his body. "Here's Tennessee in a mud puddle, sleepin' like a baby. This horse's got saddlebags stuffed full of possibles! Looks like I'm goin' to get that steel-gray after all!" he hollered. The man never saw the rifle barrel swing out of the shadows. If he had been conscious when he tumbled to the ground between the horses, he would have seen Tap's boot step on the dropped match.

The scene turned to complete darkness.

"Cow Town, is that you?"

"I'm to your left, Mase."

"Donnie-Bill, are you at the horses? Donnie-Bill!"

"This ain't good, Mase!"

"Donnie-Bill, where are you?"

"What if that gunslinger's part Indian? Them Indians is sneaky. He looked sorta dark-skinned. That daughter of his was Indian for sure."

"We should've finished 'em off down by the river."

"Don't want no part of shootin' women and kids."

"Well, someone got Donnie-Bill!"

"Maybe the horse kicked him too!"

The voices edged closer as Tap searched the ground around his boots. He found a short piece of wood about the size of his arm and tossed it into the dark on the far side of the creekbed.

"He's tryin' to get away!"

Revolvers roared. Flames flashed.

One gunman was no more than fifteen feet from Tap. On the third shot at the phantom enemy, the barrel of Tap's rifle caught the back of the man's skull and dropped him to the ground.

The other gun grew silent also.

"Mase?" came a whisper.

A year ago I would have shot all four of you without even stoppin' to see who you were. Cow Town, you're mighty lucky I'm a changed man.

"Mase, I'll meet you at the horses!" came the rasping, hurried croak.

Your horses or mine?

From the sound of the steps in the night, Tap could tell that the one called Cow Town was retreating up the creekbed. Within a few minutes he heard a horse ride east.

Well, at least he left you your horses, boys.

When Tap was convinced that the rider was well in the distance, he lit a match and examined the men on the ground. All three were still unconscious, lying facedown in the mud, sticks, and leaves. *The Pothook-H must be mighty hard up to hire bushwhackers like you. Can't figure you for a ranch crew.*

Pulling his knife from his boot, Tap cut the suspenders on the first two men and tied their hands behind their backs. The third man didn't have suspenders or a belt, but Tap discovered a large Bowie knife in a scabbard at the back neckline of the man's soiled canvas jacket. He yanked out the buckhorn knife and then pulled the man's coat up over his head, pinning it to the ground with the knife.

You might as well have a reminder of how close you came to gettin' that blade. Providin' you three don't wake up in the dark and start blastin' each other.

Tap mounted Roundhouse and rode up the creek.

And I was plannin' on makin' camp here. I have no idea where I'm headed. It's too dark to trail. Too dark to ride. Cow Town rambled east, but there's a canyon entrance to the north. The draft horse seemed to ride right up this dry creekbed. But that was before the drizzle. Even if there are some traces of tracks, I'm not going to read them until daylight.

He had gone less than a hundred yards when he thought he smelled smoke. He trailed the aroma across the creekbed to the north and into some sort of meadow. He lit a match and swung low to look at the ground.

A fire? This meadow's been burned. Maybe lightnin'. But that isn't meadow grass . . . is it?

Tap slipped down to the ground and lit another match. He plucked up a few stalks of tall plants that had escaped the fire. *Wheat? Someone's farmin' up here? The Quakers. Those boys said the Quakers got burned out at a place called Badger Crick . . . or Badger Canyon . . . Badger something. At least the crops were burned out. Where's the farmhouse?*

Tap rode north across the burned field, as his nose led him toward the source of the smoke.

There's a mouth of a small canyon up here somewhere.

The clouds began to break. A sliver of moonlight enabled him to see a few dark shadows of some structures ahead of him. A smoke column drifted up from a stovepipe that protruded out of the big white canvas roof of a half-built log house. Next to it was a shed with no roof. A little corral behind the house held some stock. Tap thought he spotted a couple of draft horses among the other animals.

His rifle across his lap, he called out to the darkened tent, "Ho, in the cabin! I come in peace, brothers. Anyone home?"

There was no reply other than the sound of milling animals in the corral.

"Friends," he called out, "I just waylaid some bushwhackers down the creek. I'm not one of them. Anyone in there I can talk to?"

Still no reply.

"Look, folks, I know you're in there. Someone has been tendin' the fire. I'm lookin' for a good friend of mine named Lorenzo Odessa. I have reason to believe he was brought this way with a couple of big draft horses after his pony was shot up on Cedar Mesa."

"Tap?" a voice called out from the tent.

"Lorenzo?"

"Just a minute—we'll be right up!"

Up? Where are you? In a basement?

"Tap, did you say you killed them bushwhackers?"

"They'll have some powerful headaches come mornin', but I didn't kill 'em."

A deep masculine voice responded, "Praise the Almighty. You didn't take a life."

A bearded man in dark overalls opened the tent flap and peered out into the night. "Welcome, friend. I'm Ezra Miller."

"And I'm Tap Andrews. I'm runnin' the Slash-Bar-4. Odessa's my foreman."

The man turned to a boy about twelve who peeked out the canvas flap that served as a front door. "Peter, put Brother Andrews's horses in the barn."

"Don't pull the saddles, son. I might need to ride in a hurry."

"Are you sure it's all right to light a lantern?" a woman's voice asked.

"Yes, ma'am. Three of 'em are laying unconscious in the mud, and the fourth hightailed it for home."

"Children, you stay down anyway," ordered the woman.

Tap stayed at the tent flap until a lantern flickered into a dim glow in the large tent-topped building. He stepped inside. The right half of the room had carpets spread across the dirt and enough furniture crammed in it to open a mercantile. The left half of the tent was an eight-foot-deep hole, a dug-out room accessible by a small wooden ladder. A woman who looked to be in her thirties, dressed in a long black dress, climbed up first.

"Please excuse the rather bizarre accommodations, Brother Andrews," the man explained. "Mrs. Miller will boil some coffee. You'll have a bite to eat, won't you?"

"I don't want to inconvenience you none, ma'am."

"Brother, if you don't let her feed you, she'll be depressed for a week."

"In that case I'd love something to eat." Tap studied the room, then called out, "Lorenzo."

"I'm down here with the young'uns, Tap. My leg's busted, and it takes me a spell to make it up the ladder.

"What's goin' on here?" Tap stepped over to help Odessa pull up into the main room. His right leg was splinted and wrapped in strips of a bed sheet.

"Let's have a cup of coffee. I'll try to explain what I know."

Tap, Lorenzo, and Ezra Miller sat at a long, narrow oak table as Mrs. Miller hurried around the iron woodstove that served as cookstove as well.

"You get shot?"

"Nope. But let me take it from the beginning. When did you pull into the ranch?"

"Monday evenin'," Tap reported.

"Well, Monday mornin' I'm ridin' circle tryin' to keep 'em bunched close to headquarters like you said, and I discovered tracks where a couple dozen head had been driven off."

"Shod or unshod ponies?"

"They were wearing shoes, all right. Why?"

Tap began to realize just how wet his clothes were as they steamed in the heat of the tent. "I ran across an Indian hoofprint out on the prairie."

"Anyway," Lorenzo continued, "I discovered some cows grazin' up on that cedar mesa."

"I gathered them yesterday," Tap informed him.

"They was still there? Good . . . that's good. I couldn't find a soul, so I began to round them up, and then a blast came out of the cedars and dropped my pony right on top of my right leg. My knee hit the rocks, and that dead bushytail parked his corpse right on top of me. I got my carbine and squeezed off a couple shots, but I was sufferin' some terrible pain. There was no way I could pull that leg out from under the horse. I expected someone to come chargin' out of the cedars to finish me off, but no one appeared."

"They just rode off?" Tap questioned.

"I reckon. Anyway, I yanked on that horse for a couple hours. Finally I got desperate and fired a shot, tryin' to attract someone's attention."

Ezra Miller stepped forward. "My son Peter and I were hunting logs and heard it."

"Huntin' logs?" Tap questioned.

"We're building our cabin, but long, straight logs are hard to find around here."

"So that's why the draft horses—to pull logs home with."

"Yes. We drug the horse off Brother Odessa and brought him to the farm."

"These folks know how to doctor a man, Tap. Couldn't have done better if I was in Dodge City." Lorenzo patted his injured leg. "Ezra was going to drive me back to the ranch in their wagon, but some bushwhackers started throwing lead into the canyon. We were waitin' it out."

Tap pushed his hat back and wiped moisture from his bushy eyebrows. "I ran into this bunch down near the river yesterday mornin'. They claim to be ranch hands at some place called the Pothook-H."

"I was told that ranch went under during the hard winter of '79," Ezra reported. "This land is open for homesteading now. According to the county records, the Pothook-H is abandoned."

"Maybe someone thought our place was abandoned too. They left the ranch gate open and the front door of the house swingin' wide."

"They did what?" Lorenzo flipped his shaggy blond hair back out of his eyes.

"Someone opened the yard gate and the front door to the house. We had cows in the yard, on the porch, and in the house when we got there."

"They didn't . . . eh, you know . . ." Lorenzo glanced at the basement. Several sets of young eyes spied up through the flickering light.

"Yep. They did. The whole place smells like a barn."

Odessa whistled. "I'll bet Pepper pitched a fit!"

"No, she was too tired. She just said that if a stall was good enough for the baby Jesus, it was good enough for Lil' Tap."

"You have a baby?" Mrs. Miller asked from the stove.

"Not for a few more weeks, but the way he's growin' in there, it seems to me the doctor could have been wrong in his guess." Tap pulled his soiled gray hat off and ran his fingers through his hair. A drop of water splashed on his ear. He glanced up to see a small, round hole in the tent above where he sat. "Those bushwhackers been shooting at your tent?"

The big man with the jet-black beard slammed his fist into his hand. "Yes. It was not enough to burn our crops right before harvest. They are trying to scare us out. The bullets sometimes catch the tent on fire, and we have to douse them with water. In the morning we will sew them up."

"They do this every night?" Tap asked.

"This was the first night since last week," Ezra Miller replied.

"I don't know who they are, but they aren't cowhands. No rancher I ever met would threaten women and children."

"We have a legal claim on this land. Everything north of the Slash-Bar-4 to the ridge of the mountains is available according to the government maps," Miller reported.

"Well, Ezra, just fire a few shots back each time. That ought to make 'em stop and think."

"Brother Andrews, we could never do that. It's not right to take up a gun against a fellow human that the Almighty has created in His image."

"Well, I didn't mean kill them. Just toss some lead in their direction. It's surprisin' how far back a man will move when lead's flyin'."

"Oh, we couldn't do that," Miller replied. "What if a bullet hit someone quite by accident? No, I can't take that chance."

"So you'll just let them fire away until they hit the wife or kids?" Tap challenged.

"The Lord is our protection. He will provide."

"Maybe He provided you with a good rifle and a box of shells," Tap suggested.

The man shook his head firmly, his face stoic.

Mrs. Miller set a plate of boiling stew and cold biscuits in front of Tap. "Thank you, ma'am. Sure am sorry these old boys won't let you alone. I should've plugged 'em when I had a chance."

"Oh, my, no!" she exclaimed. "He—I mean, we couldn't bear to have that on our conscience."

After eating for a few minutes, Tap turned to Lorenzo, then looked at Mr. and Mrs. Miller, then back at Lorenzo. "Well, partner, can you ride tonight?"

"You bring me a saddle horse?"

"Peanut."

"Let's ride."

"It's too dark to ride tonight," Mr. Miller protested. "Please stay the night."

"Thanks, brother, but I've got a wife needin' me home tomorrow, and Odessa here is gettin' married on Saturday. We better ride." Peter Miller stood by the tent flap. "Son, could you bring those two ponies around?"

The boy disappeared into the darkness.

"Ma'am," Tap said, "this is about the best-tastin' stew in the territory. You are all invited to the headquarters on Sunday afternoon for a little shindig celebratin' Lorenzo and Selena gettin' married."

"Thank you, sir, but we don't travel on the Sabbath," Miller replied.

Tap took one more bite and then stood to leave. "I understand that, brother. But do come and see us sometime. Mrs. Andrews would be delighted to talk to someone who can give her some advice on deliverin' this child."

Lorenzo gathered up his belongings and hobbled out to the yard with Tap. Mr. and Mrs. Miller stood by the tent as Andrews shoved Odessa up on the horse and then climbed up on his own mount.

Tap laid his spurs softly on Roundhouse's flanks. The horse bucked one time, then settled down to a trot into the darkness of the night.

3

When the heavy clouds finally blew east, the temperature dropped. Tap and Lorenzo arrived back at Cedar Mesa about daybreak. Huddled around a small, hot fire, they boiled coffee in their cups and warmed their fingers—and their noses.

"I've been bouncin' along on Peanut all night tryin' to figure out who was shootin' at me, Tap. If they hate me that much, how come they didn't try to finish me off? I don't have any enemies up here. I haven't been in the territory more than a couple weeks."

"Well, don't take it personal. I figure someone was tryin' to steal a few cows. You caught up with 'em, and they dropped your pony so you wouldn't follow them."

Lorenzo's streaked beard looked several days old. His bushy blond hair curled wildly out from under the well-worn wide-brimmed felt hat. "You got that right, partner. If they were wantin' to finish me off, they could've just rode out there and plugged me."

"But that doesn't tell us who opened up the yard and house."

"Nor why those old boys are so dead set at scarin' off the Quakers. Welcome to Montana Territory, Tap. I guess it's still a little wild up here."

Lorenzo's splinted leg stuck out to the side of him like a branch on a tree. Dirt caked Tap's clothes. He could feel the dried mud on his face and neck, acquired from crawling through the brush. He began to laugh.

"Okay, Andrews, where's the humor in this?" Lorenzo demanded.

"Look at us! Lorenzo Odessa and Tapadera Andrews, Montana ranchers. We both look like we've been drug behind a chuck wagon for forty miles."

"Did you think this ranchin' thing was goin' to be easy?" Lorenzo challenged.

"Nope. But I did figure we were in charge of things. So far, all I've done is run around and try to straighten out one crisis after another."

"Well, you ain't bored, are ya?"

Tap took one last swig of coffee and then poured the grounds out into the fire. "No . . . never bored. Come on, partner, let's get down the slope before Mama frets herself into labor."

"Okay, Daddy. Whew-eee! Now there's somethin' that sounds really strange."

"I'm kind of gettin' used to it myself. Your turn is comin' soon enough, Odessa."

"Well, it's goin' to be a wonderful weddin' with the groom in a splint."

"I got a pretty good idea Selena won't complain at all." Tap ambled over to Lorenzo. "Come on, Limpy, let me shove you up into the saddle."

"Yes, sir, Daddy Tap."

The sun hazed straight above the barn when Tap and Lorenzo reached headquarters. The dull rays seemed to cool the bluish gray cloudless sky. Angelita waited for them at the gate.

"Mr. Odessa, what happened to your leg?"

"That worthless pony of mine decided to die right on top of it."

Angelita swung open the gate. Both ponies promenaded through. "But what about the wedding? You can't have a wedding like that, can you?"

"I told you before, Angelita, I'm marryin' Selena. Don't you try talkin' me out of it again," Odessa teased. "You and me wouldn't work out anyway. You're too purdy, and I'm too . . . mean."

Angelita jammed her hands on her hips. "Well, that's obvious. I just can't imagine how for a minute you'd think I could see anything in the likes of you."

"Miss Angelita, you don't cut an ol' boy no slack, do ya?"

"No, I don't. And you should say, 'any slack,' not 'no slack.'"

"You know, I'm beginnin' to think I like havin' our cottage way on the other side of the barn." Lorenzo gazed in admiration at the small house.

"It won't help, because Miss Selena said I could come visit you any time I wanted!" Angelita announced. She pulled herself up behind Tap, and they rode to the big house.

Pepper lounged on a couple of pillows stuffed in an old wooden rocking chair.

"Are you two drifters lookin' for a job? Have you worked cattle before, or did you just get trampled by a herd of buffalo?"

"Miss Pepper, surely good to see you lookin' so—so—," Odessa stammered.

"Watch your language, boy. You're flirtin' with death," she warned.

"Lookin' so . . . healthy!" Odessa concluded.

"Healthy? Is that another word for fat?"

Tap dismounted and let the reins drop to the ground. "Angelita, how about you dragging me and Lorenzo out a pan of biscuits and beans? We're too dirty to eat in the house. I'll put up the horses, and then we'll tell you the whole story."

Wrapped in a long dark green apron that Angelita had to tie, untie, and retie, Pepper carried dishes to the sink. "We've got a wonderful porch all the way around the house, and already it's too cold most of the time to sit out on it. Winter's not here yet, and I'm already wishin' for spring." From the kitchen window Pepper watched the sun slip beneath the western horizon.

"You look like you're feelin' better," Tap commented.

"Yes, it's surprising how a few nights in a featherbed will perk a girl up." She meandered back toward the fireplace where Tap was stoking the fire. "This seemed like a huge abandoned land when you were gone. But with you home and Lorenzo out in the cottage, it feels as safe and secure as McCurleys' Hotel. Maybe more so. Around here I don't have strange men always trying to make silly conversation."

"You braggin' or complainin'?" Tap needled.

Pepper stuck out her tongue and then plopped down on the sofa. "Well, Mr. Rancher Man, what do we do now?"

"I've been surmisin'."

"I figured that."

Tap finished poking at the fire and stepped over next to her. "I'd like to ride into Billings in the morning early. I want to hire someone to look after the place, feed the horses, and cook for the bunkhouse crew when we have one. You know—a headquarters man. We need someone who's equally at home tossin' a flapjack or a hooley."

"A hooley?"

"A hoolihan. You know, when you rope a horse."

"I've never roped a horse in my life." She lifted her eyebrows. "Although I did lasso this Arizona drover one time!"

"Horses are tougher to rope than drovers," he chided. "You can't spin a loop 'round and 'round over your head and expect to catch a cayuse. A hoolihan is just one quick whirl and a toss at the pony. It takes skill to rope horses out of a pen."

Pepper thought about trying to sit up straight and brush down her dress. Instead she leaned her head against the sofa cushion and closed her eyes. "You think you can just ride to town and find someone like that?"

"I'm hopin', 'cause I'm not lookin' forward to us all pullin' out of here for the weddin' on Saturday. Until things settle down to a routine, I need someone here."

"Will Mr. Odessa go with you tomorrow?"

"Nope. Figure he needs to rest up for the big day Saturday. And you'll have Angelita with you. How does that sound?"

"Lonely." She faked a pout.

"I'll be home by dark, darlin'. I just can't see any other way for all of us to go to the weddin' and still keep the ranch safe."

"Angelita will want to go with you."

"It might seem strange leavin' you here alone with a lame Odessa."

"It would seem stranger leavin' me here with a healthy Odessa!" she joked.

"Well, right at the moment you do look ravishing!"

"Love is truly blind. Right at the moment I look well-ravished. Really, Tap, why don't you take Angelita? She's been scrubbing this house for three days while I watched from a chair."

"I'll ask her. . . . 'Course I don't know if she'd want to travel with me."

The high voice filtered downward from the top of the stairs like a feather on a light breeze. "I'll go!"

"Lil' darlin', I thought you were in bed."

"Obviously I'm not. Don't worry, Mama. I'll keep an eye on him and see that he stays out of trouble."

"I'm sure that should be a great comfort to me." Pepper grimaced. "But somehow sending the two of you to town seems kind of like mixing dynamite with matches. Sooner or later everything's going to blow up."

Right after daybreak Pepper waved from the window as Angelita and Tap rode saddle horses out the front gate. She thought about watching them until they rode out of sight, but the ranch house was built with a view down the slope of the mountainside almost to the river. After ten minutes of watching their backsides, Pepper returned to her sewing folded on the end of the brown leather couch.

Now, Lord, you know that I'm kind of new at this faith business. I don't know a whole lot about how You lead, but this place surely seems like home, cows in the kitchen and all. The minute I waddled in, I knew this is where we're goin' to stay.

That was what I thought about the Triple Creek Ranch down in Colorado too, but that was before I walked in this door. I just wanted to say thanks, Lord. A little over a year ago I was drinking watered-down whiskey and dancing every night at April's.

Please, Lord, let this baby be born healthy. I don't think I could handle losing another one. And then, Lord, when You come to take my Tap home, don't let him die on some far-off lonely mountain. Let it be in my arms, Lord . . . please! The only thing that scares me more than him dying is that he might die all alone.

Pepper kicked off her slippers and stared at her round, puffy toes. She wanted desperately to rub her feet, but she didn't bother to try.

Should I make this bassinet slipcase pink or blue? Maybe You could just give me a hint about this baby I've been lugging around.

No?

I didn't think so.

"Well, Lil' Tap—or Tapina," she addressed her stomach, "you are going to wake up in a boring white-sheeted bassinet."

With ruffles on the slipcase.

White ruffles.

Lorenzo toted his dinner plate to the barn, where he was repairing the saddle cut off the dead horse. Pepper ate alone and then dragged her sewing and a shawl onto the porch. Sunlight blanketed the yard. The shadows swung slightly to the east, reminding her that it was a little past noon. For the first time since they had arrived, there was absolutely no wind. She faced the southwest, watching the trail where Tap and Angelita had departed.

This is not a good habit. If the wind picks up, it will blow right in my face. But . . . I don't want to just sit around in the house. Out here the air is fresh and clean. And . . . there's some potential for something interesting to happen.

She picked up her sewing and slowly rocked back and forth.

I am not going to spend my life sitting on the porch waiting for him to come home. Once the baby comes, I'll be too busy. And I'll have to help Angelita study her schoolbooks. And I'll have a garden to tend. But today it's nice to hear the birds in the sky, feel the warm autumn sun, smell the fresh air, taste winter coming on, and watch a rider come up the drive.

A rider?

Pepper stood up to stare down the gradual slope of the mountainside. *Wonder if Lorenzo sees him? Maybe I should call him.*

Or maybe I need to relax. This is our ranch. We don't need to run.
We don't need to hide. We don't need to grab a gun.
Do we?

From two miles away she could tell he was riding a black-and-white-splotched piebald. At one mile Pepper caught the reflection of sunlight off a silver saddle horn. At one hundred feet from the gate, she saw him pull off what looked like a yellow sash and stuff it in his bedroll. When he reached the gate, she spotted the carbine lying across his lap and a thick, drooping mustache peering out from under a dirty beaver felt hat with a Montana crease.

He dismounted, opened the gate, walked his horse into the packed-dirt yard, and then shut the gate. He mounted up and rode past the barn, the bunkhouse, the cottage—and right toward her.

"Afternoon, ma'am. I'm lookin' for Mr. Tap Andrews. I was told this is his ranch."

Pepper kept her fingers busy with the needlework but repeatedly glanced up at the man. *Who does he remind me of?*

Unseen by the rider, Lorenzo Odessa hobbled toward the house, his revolver strapped to his side.

"Yes, this is his ranch. Actually it's a partnership between my husband and Stack Lowery."

"Pleased to meet you, Mrs. Andrews. My name's Sugar Dayton. I'd like to speak with your husband." The man peeked through the front window of the house.

"My husband isn't here at the moment. Perhaps you'd like to talk to Mr. Odessa, our foreman." Dayton's startled glance took in Lorenzo, who was now standing right behind him.

"You need somethin', mister?" Odessa called out, his hand resting steady on his pistol grip.

Dayton whipped around and almost yanked his revolver from the holster. "Oh! I'm, ah . . . I'm runnin' a place up in the mountains," he stammered, "and when I heard Andrews was operatin' the Slash-Bar-4, I decided to pay my respects. My brother was a friend of Tap's."

"Sorry you missed him. What's your brother's name?"

"Well, Eugene Paul is dead. He got shot in Kansas. I believe he worked with Andrews down in Silver City, New Mexico."

"Eugene Paul Dayton?" Lorenzo shook his head. "Never heard of him, and I spent a lot of years ridin' the high country down there with Tap."

"I'm sure Tap would remember Eugene Paul. Anyway, I believe some of my men had a run-in with Mr. Andrews, mistaking him for a cattle rustler or land jumper." Then Dayton looked around slowly, as if surveying the whole headquarters area. "I just wanted to apologize for their behavior."

"You obviously ain't too discerning in who you hire," Lorenzo continued.

"They do get a little carried away. But I've straightened that out," Dayton reported.

Lorenzo lifted his hat and scratched the back of his head. "Say, did you ever work for any outfits down in New Mexico?"

"The Pitchfork, the Triple-T, the B-C-Connected."

"Those are Arizona brands," Odessa challenged.

"Yeah. I was back and forth across the line. Will Tap be home soon?" Dayton pressed.

"Oh, you know how Tap is," Odessa drawled. "He could be gone ten minutes or ten days. No way of knowin'. But go pull your tack, feed your pony some grain, and grab a bite before you have to ride on. You were plannin' to ride on, weren't you?"

"Yep. Thanks for your hospitality." Dayton tipped his hat to Pepper and rode toward the barn.

Pepper watched Dayton until he was out of sight. Lorenzo limped over and sat on the steps, stretching his splinted leg out in front of him.

"Mr. Odessa, you look very nice clean-shaven," Pepper commented.

"Figured I better commence to scrub for the weddin'. I've got to be spruced up when I wear that nobby suit of Tap's. It's mighty generous of you to lend it to me."

"Tap hasn't worn it since our wedding, nor does he intend on wearing it again. Of course, he got it a little muddy that day. It brushed very clean though. Well, what do you think?"

"About the suit?"

"No. About Mr. Sugar Dayton." Pepper shifted her weight a

bit on the pillow-stuffed rocking chair. "What's he looking over our place for?"

"I don't rightly know, Miss Pepper. It's a cinch he didn't come in here jist to apologize. I'd say, lookin' at his hands and outfit, he ain't worked cows in a couple years. He had that hog leg strapped like a show-off. Not many good cowmen put silver like that on their workin' saddle. And he couldn't remember any New Mexico ranches. He's not tellin' the whole story."

"Mr. Odessa, there are some things in all of our pasts that should be kept hidden."

"Yes, ma'am, you're right about that." Odessa bent his neck around and glanced back at Pepper. "But I didn't think we should let him stay at the ranch tonight."

"I couldn't agree with you more. That's the type when he walks into the dance hall, you're hoping he finds some other girl."

Lorenzo struggled to his feet. "I'll go buddy up to him and see what I can learn." He hiked halfway across the yard and then turned back. "Miss Pepper . . . you got yourself a gun in the house?"

"Do you think I'll need it?"

"I'd feel better if you had a little protection. Until we figure this out, we've got to be cautious."

"I've got Tap's Greener loaded by the door."

"That ought to do. Just don't point both barrels at me," he urged. "I don't want nothin' to cause me to miss my own wed-din'. You know, Miss Pepper, I had a dream last night that I was late for my weddin', and Selena got so mad she up and married someone else. Don't that beat all?"

"Mr. Odessa, that is every nervous groom's nightmare."

"It is? Well . . . I figure between you, me, Tap, and little Miss Angelita, I'll get there on time one way or another."

"That you will. Now I'll go warm up some dinner for our— guest."

Pepper saw very little of Odessa or Sugar Dayton after that. Lorenzo insisted on feeding the man in the bunkhouse, informing her that "hired hands and drifters don't eat in the big house—ever." Odessa escorted Dayton on horseback to the east in the middle of the afternoon.

At sundown she was slicing apples for a pie when she was startled by a voice from the yard. "Ho, in the big house!" She expected it to be Lorenzo or even Tap and Angelita coming back from Billings. But a short man wearing a round hat stood by a tall, thin white horse.

I didn't get this many visitors when we lived in Cheyenne!

She opened the front door, stepped out on the porch, and shaded her eyes. "May I help you?"

"Evenin', ma'am. I didn't want you to go takin' no potshots at me. I'm your new bunkhouse cook and headquarters man. Is that the cookhouse over there?"

"Eh . . . yes. Did my—"

"You cookin' supper already?"

"Yes, I've—"

"Well, that's okay. But if there ain't any hands around, I can do the cookin' for you all."

"Excuse me." Wearing an apron and still holding a tea towel in her hands, Pepper walked gingerly down the steps and across the yard toward the man. "Did my husband hire you?"

"Yes, ma'am. You're Mrs. Andrews, ain't ya?"

"And you are . . ."

"Howdy Renten."

"Howdy?"

"That's my Christian name. Mama named me after the first thing my daddy said when he saw me."

"So Tap hired you today in Billings?"

"Yes, ma'am, he did. Me and Tap go back to Arizona together. I wrangled horses and cooked chuck down on the Flying 11 Ranch. Tap and me worked several roundups together. Sure was surprised to stumble across—I mean, to run into him in Billings. Told me he'd pay me a dollar and a half a day, providin' I took a bath once a week."

"Can you toss a hoolihan?" she questioned.

"Eh—yes, ma'am," Howdy affirmed.

"Good. That's very important, you know."

"Yes, ma'am."

Pepper waved her arm toward the buildings on the far side of the yard. "There's a little bedroom off the cook shack, I think. That's for you. I really haven't examined it. Our foreman, Mr. Odessa, is out on the ranch, but he'll be back soon."

"Odessa? Lorenzo Odessa? He's still alive?"

"Yes, he is."

"Don't that beat all? Did Tap ever tell you about the time I had to ride into Nogales and spring the two of them out of that Mexican jail after they got caught in Alcade's daughter's bedroom closet?"

"Eh—no, I don't think he mentioned that."

"Well . . . well . . . no. I don't reckon he would. I can tell you one thing, Mrs. Andrews." Renten spat a wad of tobacco ten feet to his left. "You got two men with sand at this ranch. They won't back away from anyone or anything. I reckon I stumbled into a mighty good layout. Yes, indeed, a mighty good layout. I'll go settle in. What time's supper?"

"I'm waiting for Tap and Angelita to return from town."

"Oh. I plum forgot! Ol' Tap ran across a little trouble in Billings. He won't be coming home tonight."

She could feel the skin around her eyes tighten. "Is he all right?"

"Oh, yeah. There wasn't much shootin' . . . nothin' serious . . . yet. A couple hombres were on the prowl. I ain't much at readin', but I think he explained it here in this letter." He pulled a long brown envelope out of his pocket and handed it to Pepper. "I'll go put Saint Peter—that's my horse—in the corral."

Pepper ripped the letter open.

> *Pepper darlin',*
>
> *First, we are both doing fine, and there's nothing to worry about. Don't tell Lorenzo, but Selena had a little trouble here in town with a couple of drifters who used to visit her at the dance hall. Do you remember Jackson and Bean? Anyway, it's nothin' I can't handle. I just*

didn't want to go off and leave her a day before her wed-
ding in a town where she hardly knows anyone.

I'm sending Howdy to look after the place. Don't let
his looks or smell fool you. He's a good man and will
back you even with his life. You see that Odessa gets all
slicked up before you two bring the wagon to town
tomorrow. Tell him I had some unexpected business in
Billings.

We have a room at the England House, but I'm stick-
ing Selena in with Angel-girl. I'll take Selena's room at the
hotel in case these two romeos try any late-night sere-
nades. It will be a great delight to get these two married
off and hide them out at the ranch where they can't get
into any more trouble.

See you in the morning, beautiful, if my heart doesn't
break of loneliness tonight.

Tap

Pepper lifted the hem of her dress and hiked back to the house.
As she closed the big oak door behind her, the place suddenly
seemed huge, cold, and very empty.

Tattered red, white, and blue banners still flagged in the wind
as Tap and Angelita rode into Billings. Less than one month earlier, railroad tycoon Henry Villard, former President U. S. Grant,
and other dignitaries had gathered at Gold Creek, north of Deer
Lodge City, and celebrated the completion of the Northern Pacific
Railroad. Saint Paul, Minnesota, and Portland, Oregon, were now
linked by a railroad.

All along the line, rail towns and tent cities gloried in the event
they assumed would bring great prosperity to their region. A large
canvas banner reading Welcome to Montana's Heartland, faded
and wind-torn, still stretched across the railroad depot.

"Maybe we should stop so I could look at the railroad depot!"
Angelita prodded.

"What? We haven't been in town two minutes, and you're

already wanting to bilk some pilgrim out of two dollars? Your days of workin' the crowd at the train depots are over, young lady."

"I just thought I'd see if I could rile you," she shot back. "You're easy to predict, Mr. Tap Andrews. Now where are we going first? How do we find someone to hire?"

"We look for the Drovers' Cafe."

"Do they have one here?"

"It might have a different name, but it's the same thing. But first we need to find Miss Selena and invite her to dinner. What would you like to eat?"

"I'd like some lobster."

"You'd like what?"

"Lobster. I read in the newspaper that the train would soon be hauling in food from the East Coast. They said the day would come when you could go into a Montana hotel and order fresh lobster. So that's what I want."

"Beefsteak is what you'll have."

"Then why did you ask me what I wanted?" she pouted.

"Come on." Tap trotted his horse to the rail in front of the New York Hotel.

He tried to brush the road dust off his jacket as he stood on the raised wooden sidewalk in front of the tallest building in Billings. Angelita, coat buttoned to her neck and wool hat pulled down to her ears, scampered into the lobby ahead of him.

The hotel felt hot and stuffy. Tap unbuttoned his coat and let it swing open as he approached the counter. Angelita was already in a heated discussion with the clerk.

"You got problems, lil' darlin'?"

"Eh," the clerk stammered, "are you with her?"

"Yep."

"Oh, well . . . I was just telling this girl . . . that, eh, Miss Selena is in Room 24."

"Thanks, mister." Tap tipped his hat.

"Actually he was just tellin' me that they didn't cater to my kind in this hotel," Angelita reported.

"He said that?"

"Yeah, but he changed his mind when you unbuttoned your coat and showed your .44," she went on. "What kind am I anyway?"

Tap stared down at her round, brown eyes and white-toothed smile. "Smart," he replied. "They obviously don't want too many smart people stayin' here at once. It would make the help look bad."

"Eh . . ." The clerk closed the registration book and dropped his pencil. "I presume you won't be needing a room?"

"Mister, you're gettin' smarter by the minute." Tap's right hand rested on the polished walnut grip of his holstered Colt. "Maybe you aren't a complete idiot."

The smile slipped off Angelita's face. "He didn't say that because I'm Mexican, did he?"

"Oh no, I'm sure that wasn't it." Tap's hand still rested on his revolver. "Was it, mister?"

"Eh . . . why, no. I, eh—it's just . . ." Beads of sweat appeared on the man's brow.

"That permanent tan of hers sure is purdy, isn't it?" Tap pressed.

"Why, certainly . . . yes! Yes, it is."

"Those pigtails probably fooled him, and he thought you were under age for checkin' into a room by yourself."

The clerk took a deep breath. "That's a good way of putting it."

"I thought so." Tap took his hand off the gun. "Now, darlin', how about you runnin' up to Room 24 to see if Miss Selena's available for dinner?"

Angelita scampered up the stairs. Tap turned to the counter. The nervous clerk had slipped into a back room. Tap wandered over to a table littered with several newspapers. The newest well-worn paper was dated April 4, 1883, St. Paul. He tossed them aside and studied a map on the lobby wall that showed the exact route of the Northern Pacific across Montana. While he stood there, several hotel patrons filtered into the lobby.

Looks like Cantrell's Siding will be the shortest route from the ranch to a railhead—if this map is right. Maybe we could ship cattle from there.

A commotion near the stairs caused him to spin around. Two men loitered at the bottom of the stairs talking loudly to Selena. Angelita stood a couple of steps behind her. Tap scooted closer.

"And I say you're comin' with us. You've got some dancin' to do!" The speaker was tall and thin and wore greasy wool pants. A dirty red bandanna ringed his neck. He also needed a shave, haircut, and clean shirt. He wore no holster, but carried a converted Navy Colt jammed into the front of his belt.

"You owe us, Selena," the shorter man insisted. He looked as if he had just walked out of a clothing store—new suit, new hat, polished black boots, oiled hair, waxed mustache. His new Colt Peacemaker was cased in a stiff brand-new leather Wyoming holster. "You shanghaied us and lifted our pokes down in Colorado. We just want what we paid for, that's all!"

Tap walked slowly across the lobby, trying to keep his spurs quiet. Several people scooted out the front door. The clerk peered out from the back room.

"I owe you nothing!" Selena insisted "I will not go anywhere with the likes of you two. If you continue to aggravate me, I have no choice but to use force."

"Force? Did you hear that, Bean?" the taller one sneered. "She's going to use force."

"I guess that means she'll pull that long, skinny knife out of her sleeve and try to stick us, like last time! It won't work, dance-hall dove. We don't scare off that easy."

Selena's dark eyes flashed. She wore a white knit shawl over her green velvet dress. Her arms were crossed and her hands buried in opposite sleeves. "I assure you, if I had pulled a knife on you before, you wouldn't be standing here badgering me."

Tap moved directly behind the men. *She probably does have her hand on that knife.*

"You're comin' with us now! I'm through talkin'!"

The man in the fancy suit awkwardly tried to pull the gun out of the new holster. Tap stepped up and smacked the man's wrist with the barrel of his .44. The new pistol crashed to the floor, and its owner let out a howl. All in one motion, Tap grabbed the other man's hair and yanked his head down until the .44 was jammed into his ear.

"Angelita, grab that pistol. Now you boys aren't quite through talkin'."

"What do you think you're doin', mister? You're interferin' in somethin' that ain't your business."

"Oh, it's my business. Miss Selena is a personal friend of mine." Tap kept his gun at the man's head. His partner clutched a badly bruised wrist.

"Shoot, she's a personal friend to ever' man between the Rockies and the Pacific. She ain't nothin' more than a common—"

Tap pulled the hammer of his revolver back two clicks. "Choose your next word very carefully, mister. Now what were you goin' to call her?"

"Eh, she's a . . . a, eh . . ."

"What's goin' on here?" a voice shouted from the doorway.

Tap turned to see a wide-shouldered man toting a shotgun and wearing a sheriff's badge.

"This drifter drew his gun on us," Bean complained, still clutching his wrist.

"Put your gun down, mister!" the sheriff shouted.

"These men insulted this lady. I will not holster my gun until they apologize," Tap asserted.

"Did they insult you, ma'am?"

"Yes, they did."

"Well, then, boys," the sheriff directed, "you better apologize to the lady . . . or else I'll just make my rounds and leave you with this hombre."

"What?"

"He said apologize," Tap growled. "Perhaps you mistook Miss Selena for some other woman."

The men glanced at each other and then at Selena. "Yeah," Bean blurted out. "Sorry, ma'am, we must have mistook you for someone else. Didn't we, Jackson?"

The one with Tap's gun shoved in his ear nodded slightly. "Yeah," he mumbled.

"Just make sure it doesn't happen again," Selena demanded.

Tap released his grip on Jackson. "Give him his pistol, Angelita."

"I was hoping to sell it at the depot for four dollars," she grumbled, handing it back to the man.

"Four? I paid sixteen cash dollars for this outfit."

"What a waste." Angelita shrugged.

"Come on, you two . . . out of the hotel!" the sheriff commanded.

"We'll be around town, mister," Jackson hissed to Tap. "We aim to see you again."

"That would be a great mistake," Tap assured him.

When the two men had left, the sheriff confronted Tap. "Mister, I don't know who you are, but I don't want any trouble out of you. Leave that .44 in the holster. If you have difficulty, you come look me up. But if you start pullin' that gun ever' time you walk into a building, I'll have you locked up within the hour. Do you savvy?"

"Yeah, I understand. But if those two come after me with drawn guns, I'm goin' to protect myself—and these womenfolk."

"I'll do the protectin' around here," the sheriff insisted.

Tap nodded his head and jammed the revolver back into his holster.

The restaurant at the England House did not list lobster on the bill of fare. Selena, Angelita, and Tap sat at a corner table and finished a meal of beefsteak, boiled red potatoes, gravy, and beets. The coffee was pitch-black and thick. It took Tap three cups before he decided he liked it.

Selena listened as Tap explained the situation at the ranch and Lorenzo's broken leg.

"This is the dumbest thing I ever heard of. He's out there getting into trouble. I'm in here and trouble is searching me out. Why aren't we together? Why did we have to wait for this . . . wedding?"

"Because it's the proper way to do things," Tap reminded her.

"Well, why do I need to do things proper?"

"Because you are no longer the Selena those two old boys are lookin' for, right?"

Selena's dark eyes blazed, and then a smile broke across her smooth but seasoned face. "Okay, Andrews. You win. This time. Besides, I only have to wait until tomorrow. Not much can go wrong between now and then, can it?"

Tap glanced at Angelita. She raised her thick black eyebrows and rolled her eyes to the ceiling.

After the meal, Tap walked Selena and Angelita back to the New York Hotel. Then he proceeded to survey the town on foot. It didn't take him long to discover the Bear Cub Saloon and Cafe. A quick look around the crowded, narrow room, and Tap knew he was in the right place. These weren't prospectors, Easterners, nor store clerks. A Friday afternoon room full of drifters, cow-punchers, gamblers, and horse thieves. It was Tap's kind of place.

The bartender looked twice when Tap ordered coffee but came back and leaned against the polished mahogany bar with a cup of coffee for himself as well. Tap figured the man was six inches taller and about a hundred pounds heavier than himself. The bartender stooped and put his elbows on the bar and looked Tap in the eyes. "If you ain't goin' to get soused and you ain't eatin', have you got somethin' else in mind?"

"I just took over the Slash-Bar-4 and need someone to cook chuck and baby-sit the stock at the headquarters. How many of these boys have some cow sense?"

"Most of 'em have herded bovines." The bartender stood and straightened the black bow tie that encircled his massive, collar-incased neck. "'Course it wasn't always their own beef they was chasin'. Most of the good hands are workin' the roundups north and west of here. You say you want a cowman or a yard man?"

"Well, to start with—a yard man."

"I don't think there's an hombre in here that could cook worth spit. But I do know one old boy who fits the bill. Comes in here ever' night and orders a beer, then sits in the corner and plays solitaire. Smells like a skunk, but his two bits is as good as the next man's. I heard some of the boys say he drove a chuck wagon all the way from El Paso and never took a bath once. So I guess he can cook."

"Plays solitaire? Does he talk real loud when he plays?" Tap asked.

"Yep."

"Wears a round hat and rides a tall white horse?"

"That's him."

"Where's he stayin'?"

"Smellin' like that, he surely don't have a room," the bartender chuckled. "Must be camped out along the river. All I know is, I expect he'll be here right after suppertime."

"If he comes in, tell him to wait right here. I'm lookin' for him."

"What's your name, mister?"

"Tap Andrews."

The man flinched when he heard the name, but Tap didn't bother asking why. He finished his coffee and left the crowded, noisy, smoky room. He rode Roundhouse out along the tracks to the river looking for a tall white horse and a stoop-shouldered man wearing a round, floppy hat. He found neither.

Tap rode every street more than once before he spotted the white horse parked by itself on a rail in front of the El Dorado Club. Most of the tables still had chairs stacked on top when he pushed open the tall, narrow doors and stepped inside. The room had a fifteen-foot-high ceiling and a bar that ran the entire length of the room. On the wall behind the bar hung a twenty-foot picture of a reclining woman.

Peering around the stacked chairs, Tap spotted a man sitting alone in the far corner of the room with his back to the wall, a deck of cards spread on the table in front of him. The man mumbled something about the ace of clubs.

"Don't look under that jack of clubs!" Tap called out. "That's cheatin'!"

The man's head shot up so quickly that he rammed his knees into the table. He grabbed at a teetering amber bottle. "You almost made me spill my . . ." The man cocked his head sideways. "Tap? Did I die and go to Hades? I thought you was dead."

"I'm not dead, Howdy, and I don't aim to go to Hades when I am. What are you doin' in Montana?" Tap pulled up a chair, turned it backwards, and plopped down next to the older man.

"Me? I come up here with the O-Bar-O . . . wasted my money . . . and got stuck in this railroad town. But what about you? You're supposed to be rottin' at A.T.P. Last I heard the Yaquis shot you down east of Yuma."

"Ever'thing's changed. I'm a married man with a baby on the way, runnin' a big Montana ranch."

"Are you sure you're the real Tap Andrews?"

"Oh, it's me, Howdy."

"Well, I'll be! You hirin'?"

"I need a bunkhouse cook and a headquarters man. A dollar and a half a day, but you only get paid if you've had a bath," Tap insisted.

"Ever' month?"

"Ever' week."

"A bath ever' week! Even in the winter? That could kill a man."

"You want the job or not?"

Howdy pushed the cards into a pile in front of him. "When do I start?"

"I need you to mount that skinny white horse of yours and ride to the ranch right now. Go get your belongin's and meet me back here in ten minutes."

"I'm wearin' my belongin's."

Tap pushed his hat back and scratched his head. "Come on then, Renten. I'll draw you a map to the ranch."

Both men hiked across the wooden floor. Tap's spurs jingled as his boots banged the bare wood. He followed Renten down the stairs to the hitching rail. Then he leaned against a post that held the roof above the wooden boardwalk in front of the El Dorado Club.

The shot seemed to come from the roof of the building across the street. It shattered the wooden four-by-four only a foot from Tap's head. Pulling his pistol as he dove to the dirt, he rolled to his knees behind the hitching rail. A second blast stirred up dirt behind Roundhouse.

The big gray gelding yanked free from the rail and bucked his way down the street. Renten's horse danced, panicked, and pushed Howdy back to the wooden stairs.

Tap's shot slammed into the ledge along the roof line of the two-story wooden building across the street. Whoever had been there now cowered for cover.

The roar of the sheriff's shotgun silenced the shootout.

4

Mister," the sheriff roared, "I warned you before. I don't want that gun comin' out of the holster!"

Tap refused to look at the lawman. He scanned the roof line for signs of his attacker.

"Did you hear me, mister?"

Renten settled his horse down and retied him at the rail. "Somebody took a shot at him, Sheriff."

"Drop it in the dirt! Just drop the gun!" The sheriff approached Tap one slow step at a time.

Convinced that the gunman or gunmen had fled, Tap released the hammer on his Colt but kept it in his right hand. "I'm not dropping my gun in the dirt. I spent an hour last night cleanin' it. But I will holster it." Tap shoved the gun back into the holster and turned to face the man.

"Pull that holster and hand it to me," the sheriff commanded. "I'm taking your gun until you're ready to leave town."

"Why ain't ya chasin' down them guys that tried to bushwhack us?" Renten called out.

"I'll disarm them when I catch up with them. Right now I want *your* gun!"

"You expect me to waltz around town unarmed with someone on the prowl?"

"They aren't going to shoot an unarmed man. Did you see who it was?"

"I reckon it was the ones from the New York Hotel."

"I didn't ask you what you reckon. I asked if you saw who it was."

"No, I didn't see them."

"The gun!" the sheriff demanded.

Tap pulled his holster off and handed it to the sheriff.

"You get in another scrape, and I'll jail you."

"If I get in another scrape without my gun, I'll be dead," Tap fumed.

"Mister, we're building a nice town here, a town of honest folks, hard-workin' ranchers and farmers. Someday Billings will be the capital city of the state of Montana. We don't need any riffraff blowin' into town and shootin' it up. Your kind can just move on."

"Afraid you'll have to put up with me. I'm here to stay." Tap searched the man's eyes. *Six months. He'll either quit or be dead in six months. He's just not the lawman type.*

"Tap here is runnin' a big ranch."

"Oh, yeah? Which place is that?" the sheriff asked.

"The Slash-Bar-4." Tap's eyes still searched the street for signs of the two men he had encountered at the hotel.

"The Slash-Bar-4?" The sheriff bristled. "That was my ranch before the bank took it back!"

Tap watched as the sheriff continued to point the shotgun at him. "Well, it's not your ranch now. It was bought outright by a Mr. Lowery. I'm runnin' the place as a partner."

"You rich bulls think you can come in here and buy up the territory," the sheriff growled.

"Mister, don't let your past affect the way you do the job, or you won't be sheriffin' very long."

"I don't need advice from some carpetbagger!"

Tap glanced over at Howdy, then back at the sheriff. "Don't you have somethin' better to do than aggravate citizens?"

"Don't try anything else in this town. I'm warning you!"

"You took away my pistol, and you warned me. I've got nothin' else to say to you!" Tap turned and walked away.

"Where are you goin'?"

"To chase down my horse, providin' someone hasn't shot it already!"

Howdy Renten mounted up his horse and rode alongside Tap as he searched the streets and alleys. They found Roundhouse at a water trough behind the England House Hotel.

"You figure on chasin' them boys down?"

"I don't know where they are, who they are—and don't have my gun. I think I'll let them come to me. I assume they were the ones I backed down at the hotel."

"You headin' back to the ranch then?"

"Nope, there's a little too much excitement here. I'm going to stay overnight. You're going to the ranch. Let me draw you a map to the place, and I'll give you a note for Pepper."

"Your wife's named Pepper?"

"Yep."

"Tapadera Andrews a family man! I still can't figure it." Half the tobacco spit flew across the street from Renten's lips. The other half dripped across his chin onto his vest.

The thin, narrow-eyed clerk at the New York Hotel scooted into the back room the minute Tap entered the lobby. Even on this cool autumn day, Tap's boiled shirt felt sweaty under his canvas jacket as he bounded up the stairs and rapped on the door marked #24.

He waited a moment, then knocked again. "Selena? Angelita?"

The white door with painted gold trim opened about an inch. A big, round brown eye stared out at him.

"I'm sorry, but we're not allowed to have gentlemen callers in our room."

"That's no problem, ma'am," Tap laughed. "I'm not a gentleman."

"Oh, well, in that case . . ." Angelita swung open the door.

"You two ladies all right? You haven't had any more trouble?"

Selena sat in a padded wooden chair in front of the dresser mirror combing her long, dark hair. "Oh, we're fine," she replied. "We've been sitting here discussing men, marriage—things like that."

"Good." Tap winked at Selena. "I hope you've taught her a thing or two."

"Yes, I have," Angelita piped up. "She's a quick learner. Did you know that Miss Selena is half-Mexican?"

"Yep. I did know that. Have you had any more hassles from those two old boys that were down in the lobby?"

"No. How about you?"

"Well, someone took a couple of potshots at me. The sheriff took away my pistol. Other than that, it's been fairly dull. Oh . . . I did hire a yard man."

"Then are we going back to the ranch now?" Angelita asked.

"No. I took a room at the England House. I want you two to spend the night there. I'll take Selena's room in case your admirers try to stir up trouble."

"What will you do without a gun?" Angelita asked.

"Bite 'em." He reached over and patted her shoulder.

"Did you want me to pack all my things?" Selena asked.

"Nope. Just take what you'll need until mornin'. We'll stroll around town like we're shoppin' and then eat supper at the England House. How well do you know those two men? Are they goin' to try somethin' else dumb?"

"The one with the new suit is called Bean. The other is called Jack, I think. They rode with a big Swede named Wild Dog. But I don't know much else. A lot of men came to April's, and I've tried to forget most of them." Selena began to put her hair up in combs. "'Course I do remember the first time you came to April's." She didn't look back at Tap.

"Was Mrs. Andrews working there then?" Angelita asked.

"Oh, no. She and I had a little disagreement over a few dollars and a sharp knife. She quit to go huntin' for a Colorado rancher for a husband."

"Was that you, Mr. Andrews?" Angelita asked.

"Not exactly. But I do remember sittin' in the kitchen at April's eatin' some horrible burnt eggs with Stack Lowery when Selena first came in, bruised and battered."

"Did you have a wreck?" Angelita asked.

"Yeah, I ran into a man's fist—several times. I think that was a few days before Tap saved my life the first time."

"He did?" Angelita's brown eyes grew bigger.

"Sure. Didn't you know that's his mission in life? He goes from

town to town saving women's lives, especially those who keep gettin' beat up."

"He does?"

"Selena's gettin' carried away," Tap demurred.

"Angelita, listen to me," Selena lectured. "In life there are two
kinds of men. Those that will protect you and those that will hurt
you. The sooner you learn how to tell which is which, the better
off you are. And Tap here . . . well, he's pretty easy to read. He,
Stack, Lorenzo—they're cut from the same mold that way. They'll
stay by you and protect you with their lives, if need be. That's the
kind you marry. Especially in a wild country like this."

"Marry?" Tap objected. "Angelita promised me she wasn't gettin' married for twenty years!"

Angelita revealed her straight white teeth in a wide grin. "He's
extremely possessive."

Tap slumped in the dark of Selena's room at the New York
Hotel. A blanket was pulled up to his chin like a barber's sheet.
Across the room the brass bedstead was empty.

Empty of people.

The pillows were arranged like a body, and the thick covers
were pulled over the top.

All except one blanket.

He sat silently for a good hour.

*It's a cat-and-mouse game. Only I'm not sure if I'm a cat or a
mouse. If those two are lookin' for me, they won't come here. But
if they can't find me, maybe they'll come lookin' for Selena—and
I'll be waitin'. 'Course they might be stone-drunk and lying under
a poker table in some saloon. Or at the dance hall. Or maybe they
just took a shot at me on their way out of town. They could be
halfway to Miles City . . . or Bozeman.*

*'Course I didn't see them take those shots at me. Reckon that
could have been someone else. Which is a cheery thought. Lord,
what am I doin' here anyway? I ought to be with Pepper. I should
never have come to town. After this weddin' I'll send Odessa in
on the errands. If I stay at the ranch, I'll keep out of trouble.*

Lord, I babble a lot when I get tired. Especially when the room is stuffy and smells like perfume.

Lord, take care of Pepper. And Angelita. And Selena.

He figured a fifteen-minute nap would do him a lot of good.

A two-hour nap was even better. . . . He woke up with a very stiff neck, hearing a scratching, rattling sound that seemed to come from the window.

Well, it's comfortin' to know you boys are predictable.

A loud rap sounded on the door.

I open the front door while the other sneaks in the window? Come on, boys, you can do better.

Tap waited until the one at the door called out, "Selena, I need to talk to you. I want to apologize for my earlier behavior." Then Tap scooted toward the door in his stocking feet, the blanket still wrapped around his shoulders.

"Open up, Selena. It's me—Bean. I've got money this time!"

Tap turned the cold brass knob on the door and swung the door open into the darkened room a couple of inches. He could hear Jackson tug to raise the warped window.

Bean stuck his head in. "Jackson's not with me. All that this afternoon was his idee." He stepped toward the bed. "Miss Selena?"

The iron doorstop was in the shape of a duck decoy. The part that crashed into the back of Bean's head was flat and cloth-covered so it wouldn't scratch the hardwood floor. Bean didn't seem to appreciate that consideration as he dropped to the floor—unconscious.

"Bean?" Jackson called, as he straddled the window, half in, half out.

Tap squatted down, slid Bean's revolver from its new leather holster, and then crawled toward the bed.

Jackson struck a match. "Bean?" he whispered. "She's still in bed! Bean, what happened?"

His gun was drawn. In the excitement, in the darkness, Jackson had only pulled the single-action Colt to the first click. His thumb was on the hammer when he heard the second click.

But not from his gun.

From the one behind his ear.

"Don't bother turnin' around, Jackson. Just drop the gun on the floor," Tap ordered.

"You! What are you doin' here?"

"Target shootin'. But it's a mighty tame challenge with you two. Like ducks on a pond."

"You can't shoot us!"

"Sure I can. You broke into my room, didn't you?"

"Your room? This is Miss Selena's room."

"You think it's all right to break into a lady's room?"

"Selena ain't no lady! She's a—"

The barrel of Tap's borrowed revolver crashed down on Jackson's head. The man dropped to the floor beside Bean.

I didn't need to do that, Lord. Selena's right. I just can't stand it when they run a woman down. Never could. You've got to help me act different. When they get started like that, somethin' inside me lets loose. I know there's got to be a better way.

I just can't think of one.

An unconscious 180-pound man weighs a ton. Especially when you have to carry him out the window, across the roof, and down the ladder to the alley.

Double that when there are two of them. It was almost daylight by the time Tap completed the job and crawled through the window back into Selena's room. He lit the kerosene lamp and poured water into the basin. After scrubbing his face, neck, hands, and arms, he pulled his razor out of his saddlebag and shaved. Leaning close to the mirror, he could see the creases around his eyes. He noticed several flecks of gray hair on the left side of his head.

You're gettin' too old for this, Andrews. Time to retire to the ranch. Just get this weddin' over with.

He splashed his clean-shaven face with a little water.

All right, Mr. Tapadera Andrews . . . that's about the best you can do. At least you're cleaner than you were on your own weddin' day.

Tap hiked down the stairs of the New York Hotel carrying saddlebags and rifle in his right hand and a big bundle of clothing in his left. Stopping by the livery, he left his gear with his saddle and headed to the sheriff's office.

A groggy sheriff's deputy finally came to the door, barefooted and hatless, after several minutes of Tap's banging on the door.

"The office is closed. What do you want?"

"Jackson and Bean are in the alley between the hotel and—"

"Are they dead?"

"No. The sheriff took away my gun. But when they wake up, they'll have some bad headaches. They're tied back to back wearin' nothing but their long johns."

"Their what?"

"Here's their gear . . . and their sidearms. I'd greatly appreciate it if you would just hold the belongin's here until they come lookin' for 'em."

"How did you—"

"I got some help from a duck."

"You got help from where?"

"Don't worry about it. I'll be by about 2:00 for my gun."

"You leavin' town?"

"Yep, but first we've got a weddin' to take care of. Can you keep ahold of those two revolvers until I leave town?"

"Yeah, we'll keep 'em until they ride out. You know, mister," the deputy drawled, "we're goin' to be mighty happy to see you go."

"So am I, partner . . . so am I."

Tap ate a late breakfast with Selena and Angelita at the England House. Then he walked them to the New York Hotel. He inspected the alley. Jackson and Bean were gone.

There's nothin' I need to do in this town except wait for Pepper and Lorenzo. They should roll in around noon. They'll stop at the livery. I might as well wait for them there. Besides, it'll keep me out of trouble.

The livery owner, a big Dutchman, was saddling a tall black gelding as Tap approached. "Mr. Vanderwyck, I need to catch up on some sleep. Can I panhandle a corner of the loft for a nap?"

"Are you an honest, God-fearin' man?" Vanderwyck boomed.

Tap stared at the man's round face and eyes, trying to figure out the nature of the question. "Don't know where you're comin' from, but me and the Lord have things squared up, if that's what you mean. But what does that have to do with a nap in your barn?"

"I've got an emergency. Folks rented a rig this morning, and it got away from them up in the hills. I've got to go chase it down. I hired a new man to help out. This was to be his first day, but he didn't show. Too much rotgut whiskey, I reckon. I don't have time to go find him. Can I get you to watch the place until noon? We'll call your livery bill a wash."

"You got it, partner. Go on, catch your ponies. If you aren't back by 12:30, I've got to close the door and walk off. Got a weddin' to attend."

"That's fair enough. I'm obliged to you, mister. . . . Eh, what was your name?"

"Andrews. Tap Andrews. What should I do if your helper shows up?"

"Tell him he's fired."

The Dutchman mounted the saddle horse and then rode over to him. He leaned over and stuck out his massive, callused hand. "Take good care of the place. And thanks."

Tap strolled back into the barn. The office was a small room just inside the door to the left. The door stood open. Ledgers were scattered across the desk. Keys hung on a peg near the door. The upper left-hand drawer of the battered oak desk was pulled open. He glanced into the drawer. An open cigar box revealed gold eagle coins and folded greenbacks. He closed the box, slid the drawer shut, and closed the office door behind him.

He checked on Onespot and Roundhouse and then climbed into the loft, opened the big front doors, and lay back on a stack of hay.

Now don't get yourself dirty, Andrews. You've got to stand up for Lorenzo and Selena. They deserve to have you clean. 'Course that's what you said about your own weddin'.

You know, Lord, there's a lot about this Western country that I like. Men like Vanderwyck. He asks if you're God-fearin', shakes hands, and rides off leaving the business and cash box. Bet they don't do that back in the States.

That's the way it ought to be. Neighbors helpin' neighbors. Ever'one treatin' the other man square. It doesn't happen near often enough. But when it does, it feels good. I'd like to run the ranch that way.

Pay and bonuses for the hired men.

Cut of the herd to the foreman.

Meal and a bed to those in need.

I don't need to make a lot of money, Lord. Just enough to live right. And maybe a little extra to help build a school or a church. That's what I want out of this ranch deal.

'Course I reckon that's pretty much all anyone wants.

The hay was soft. Even with the upper door open, the barn walls blocked the chill of the October air. Two weeks of fitful sleep. It all rolled together and hit Tap in the middle of his ranch philosophizing.

"Hey, does anyone work here? What kind of business is this?"

Tap woke up in Arizona.

Or Colorado.

Or Wyoming.

"You've got a customer out here!"

Montana! Come on, Andrews. You promised Vanderwyck.

"I'll be right down!" he called out.

Reaching the top of the ladder to the barn floor, Tap spotted a dark-complected man with thick, drooping mustache and stove-top-crowned, round black hat. He had a holster reversed on the right side and a Bowie knife slung on the left. His wool vest was buttoned tight at the top next to his ruffled tie.

As Tap's boot heels spur-jingled to the ground, he could see a brightly painted drummer's wagon parked in front of the livery. *"Dr. Antoine Bejeaux's Famous Female Remedy." This ol' boy must be a smooth talker to get anyone to buy that stuff.*

"Are you Vanderwyck?" the man asked. "I want to talk to someone who knows horses, not just to a flunky."

"Are you Dr. Antoine Bejeaux, the famous medicinal expert from New Orleans?"

"Huh? What? . . . Oh, yes, certainly. . . . So you've heard of me?"

"Come on, Doc, ever'body in the West has heard of your Famous Female Remedy. Now what can I do for you?" *That ought to get him thinkin'. Anyone named Bejeaux has to be from somewhere in south Louisiana.*

"Oh, my . . . well." The man looked Tap up and down. "Say, I don't have a distributor in Billings yet. I just pulled into town, in fact. I'll give you first crack at the whole territory."

"Doc, I couldn't do that. Not enough women come into the livery."

Bejeaux stepped closer to Andrews. "Just between you and me, the Female Remedy makes excellent horse liniment."

"Sorry. Can't help you there. Did you have some livery business?" Tap walked with the man toward the wagon.

Bejeaux hung his thumbs in his belt. "Mister, I'm about to make you the best deal you'll have this year. Two days back I stopped at a homestead near the Dakota line. I did some business, but they were cash poor. So I traded for a foal. Well, yesterday I pull into a ranch, and what do you suppose? They want to trade me another yearling. Now what am I going to do with two ponies—even though they are obvious champions."

Tap pushed his hat to the back of his head and strolled to the back of the wagon where the young horses were tied. "So you want to sell them, do you?"

"That's right. I've got a dynamite deal for you."

Oh, I bet you do.

The long-legged palomino colt sported three white socks and a thick flaxen mane and tail.

"Well, junior, how are you doin'?" he asked the horse. "Gettin' kind of tired of trailin' a dusty wagon? Probably miss your mama a little." He stroked the colt's back. "Can you give me a foot?" Tap slid his hand down the horse's legs. Immediately the colt lifted his hoof. "That-a-boy." Tap stepped around and looked the colt in the eyes. *Someone's been takin' mighty good care of you. I could train you for a couple years. Then Lil' Tap will be ready to ride.*

"He's a beauty, isn't he?" Bejeaux offered. "Figured I'd get top money for him over in the gold fields, but I don't want to baby-sit him for weeks before I get there."

"Well, junior," Tap continued talking to the horse, "at least you weren't stuck back here by yourself. This cute, little skewbald filly made you mind your manners, didn't she?"

Tap stepped over to the other yearling, a brown and white bald-faced pinto. She was not as tall as the colt and tried to pull away from Tap.

"You a little nervous, darlin'? That's okay. It's a scary world," Tap said as he stroked her neck. "Especially for a young lady out on her own for the first time."

The filly wouldn't give Tap her foot, but she did allow him to look at her teeth and stare into her eyes.

"What are you lookin' for?" Bejeaux asked.

"Their sand."

"Their what?"

"Their sand—grit . . . determination . . . courage. That's how you can tell if they're naturally mean or just scared to death. You can tell if they'll run or stand by your side. You can tell if they'll push through a stormy night just because you ask them to."

"You can tell all of that by looking a horse in the eyes?"

"Yep."

"Well, what's the verdict? Do you want to buy the horses?"

"It sure isn't like buying a finished horse. They'll need lots of work. But I might be interested if you give me an honest price."

"Mister," the drummer began, "you being an expert horseman and a local fellow know that I could pull in fifty or sixty dollars for each when I reach the mines. But I'm not a greedy man. If you buy them both, I'll let you have them for twenty-five each. That's half price and you know it."

"Twenty-five?" Tap shook his head. "Mister, you can buy any horse in this town for twenty-five—including my own personal mount." *Especially my horse!*

"These, of course, aren't just any old horses. I believe their breeding and conformation demonstrate their quality."

"I'll give you ten dollars for the colt. The filly's too anxious," Tap offered.

The drummer stepped back and looked up at the faded painted sign on the front of the building. "That does say Livery, doesn't it? Perhaps someone else here buys the horses. Ten dollars wouldn't even cover my expenses."

"Mister, look into my eyes!" Tap demanded.

"What?"

"Look me in the eyes. It's like lookin' at a horse. Now I'm goin' to tell you somethin'. That colt is worth ten dollars, tops. I'm offerin' to give you ten. I will not give you twenty-five, fifteen, or even eleven."

Bejeaux turned back toward the foals. "You're trying to steal these fine horses."

"They aren't fine horses—yet. And if you drag them behind your wagon, they won't make it to the mine fields. I said ten and I meant it. Don't waste any more of my time."

Bejeaux started toward his wagon, then turned back. "I'm crazy for sayin' this . . . but, well, twenty-five for the two of 'em."

What am I going to do with a shy filly—even if she is a pretty horse? Maybe green-break her next year and sell her. "Mister, I've got other things to do. I'll give you eighteen for the pair."

"Let's split the difference," Bejeaux offered. "Twenty-two."

Tap waved his arms in disgust. "I'll need you to move the wagon. You're blockin' my drive." He turned around and sauntered toward the barn door.

One—two—three—four—

"Mister, did you ever sell patent medicines?" Bejeaux called out. "You'd be a natural. You're breakin' my heart. Come on, come get these ponies for twenty dollars."

Tap didn't bother turning around. *Five—six—seven—eight—nine—*

"All right . . . eighteen! Come get them before I go completely delirious and sell my whole rig for a dime."

Tap stopped in his tracks and shielded his wide grin. *I knew he would. I could see it in his eyes.*

He led the colt into the smallest corral and turned him loose. The little palomino stood by the gate and stared out under the top rail. Then Tap led the filly to the corral. When he loosened the rope, she immediately sprinted for the farthest corner of the corral and hid her head against the faded barn wall.

Antoine Bejeaux had crawled up into the wagon. Tap handed him a gold twenty-dollar double eagle.

"Keep the change," Tap offered.

"What?"

"They're worth ten dollars each. Keep the whole twenty. I trust you're better at sellin' patent medicine than you are horses. I'll need you to sign a bill of sale. Wait here and I'll go get one."

Within three minutes, the wagon rolled and rattled down the street. Tap walked back to the corral to look at the two horses. The colt scampered to greet him and searched for a treat. The filly refused to leave the far side of the corral.

"Well, you two, now I have to explain to Mama why I spent twenty cash dollars on ponies when we have a cavvy of 'em out at the ranch. I'll just tell her there's one for Lil' Tap and one for Tapina. And she'll say, 'If you think I'm ever going through this again, you are a very deluded man!'"

Tap hiked back to Vanderwyck's office. He swung the door closed, pulled off his canvas coat and hung it on a chair, and began to brush straw off of it with his hand.

Pepper wants me all purdied up.

He glanced into a broken fragment of a mirror on the wall next to a faded poster of a big black stallion.

Andrews, you're about as purdy as a tree stump in a hay field!

"Mr. Vanderwyck, I'm sorry I'm late for work. I was bush-whacked. Unavoidedly detained!"

Tap swung open the door and stepped into the barn.

"You!" Bean shouted. "Where's Vanderwyck?"

"He left me in charge. Said you were fired."

Bean's round hat was pushed back, revealing a large blue-black lump. He reached down to his side, but there was no fancy tooled leather holster. And no gun.

Bean reached to the back of his belt and yanked out a knife. "Mister, this is the last time I'm dealin' with you. This time you're a dead man!"

"Bean, surely you have something better to do than get yourself hurt again."

Tap heard the muted sound of slow-moving spurs to his right.

He stepped that way just as Bean lunged at him with the knife. He dove to the dirt of the barn floor and rolled to his back just in time to see Jackson try to hold back with the shovel handle that had been aimed at Tap's head. Instead, it crashed into Bean's shoulder, causing the knife to fly to the ground.

Tap scampered to his feet. The knife, blade first, pegged the toe of Bean's polished black shoes.

"I stabbed myself!" he screamed. "You purtneer broke my shoulder blade and made me stab myself!"

Lifting the shovel handle, Jackson lunged toward Tap. "I'm goin' to kill you!" he shouted. "You coldcocked us and left us in the alley."

Tap backed toward a stall, avoiding the swinging shovel handle. "I also stripped you and tied you up. My only mistake was not shootin' you both. Now get out of here before I get riled. You two are like crazy horseflies that won't leave well enough alone. Get out of here!"

"We ain't goin' nowhere!" Jackson snarled, lunging again. Tap dodged and came up beside Jackson and slammed his locked hands into the middle of the man's back. Jackson stumbled, face first, into the muck of the barn floor. "Knife him, Bean!" Jackson called out as he struggled to his feet.

"I cain't. I'm bleedin' to death," Bean cried. He seemed frozen in place, the knife still piercing the blood-stained black shoe. "I'm goin' to die right here, and I ain't never seen San Francisco."

Keeping an eye on Jackson as the man tried to regain his breath, Tap walked over to Bean and stepped on the toe of the injured foot. Bean let out a curse and scream, but stood in helpless fear and pain as Tap bent over and yanked the knife out of his foot.

"Stuff your bandanna in there and get yourself to a doc, Bean. It didn't go in very far."

"I'll kill you!" Bean shrieked as he dropped to the dirt. He flailed frantically at the bandanna in his back pocket.

The shovel handle caught Tap in the small of the back. A mind-numbing pain shot straight up to the back of his neck. The knife dropped as he staggered forward, trying to avoid another blow. When he spun around, Bean was limping toward him, knife in hand, and Jackson had the shovel handle raised over his head.

"Okay . . . that's it," Tap hollered. "There's nothin' a man can do with rabid skunks but kill 'em." Yanking a horse collar off a peg on a post, Tap charged a startled Jackson. The shovel handle bounced off the horse collar. Tap's fist slammed into the man's stomach with a thud. The second blow cracked like a thick stick breaking in two, catching the man on his jawbone. Jackson slumped to his knees, clutching his head in both hands.

The bloody knife blade ripped through the right arm of Tap's shirt. The gray cotton cloth gaped open, and a thin line of blood popped out, trickling onto his shirt. The horse collar caught Bean in the nose with such force that Tap instantly knew it was broken.

"Drop the knife, Bean!" he growled.

The man clutched his bleeding nose with his left hand and swung wildly at Tap with his knife-wielding right hand. This time the horse collar slammed into Bean's ear. He crumpled to the ground. Whipping around, Tap shielded his head from a blow he expected from Jackson, but the shovel handle cracked into his shins instead.

Tap collapsed to the dirt, pinning the shovel handle beneath his throbbing legs. Both men rose to their knees. Tap's right cross slammed into Jackson's chin, and the left uppercut laid him flat on his back. Jackson struggled to prop himself up on one elbow, but Tap's roundhouse caught him in the mouth. This time when Jackson hit dirt, he didn't move.

"What are you doin', Andrews? Takin' 'em on two at a time on your knees?"

Panting for breath, blood seeping down his left arm, dirt from head to toe, Tap reached for his hat. "Stack! What are you doin' here?"

"Watchin' a fight," the tall, well-dressed man replied. "'Course it wasn't much of one."

"How long you been there?"

"Since you took that blade to the arm."

"And you didn't step in to help?"

Lowery flashed Tap a full-toothed grin. "You didn't need no help, did you, Andrews?"

Tap tried to stand but collapsed to his knees. "Nah . . . I had 'em from the first blow." He reached up and took Stack's arm. The former dance hall piano player and bouncer yanked him to his feet.

"Good. I didn't want to get my suit messed up. I've got a wed-din' to go to."

"You came in for Lorenzo's weddin'?" Tap asked.

"I came in for Miss Selena's weddin'. She's one of my girls, you know."

"The weddin'! Pepper will be here, and look at me!"

"Ain't much different than your own weddin'," Stack laughed. "Listen, Andrews, I hope you ain't offended, but if I ever get married, Pepper's invited, but you have to stay at the ranch."

"You got a prospect lined up?" Tap joshed.

"At least a man can hope."

"Especially a man who owns a gold mine."

"Half a gold mine," Stack corrected.

Regaining a little strength in his throbbing legs, Tap wobbled beside the towering Stack Lowery out of the livery. A black leather carriage pulled by matching sixteen-hand black geldings waited in the street.

"Nice rig."

"Just bought it," Stack related. "Had it and the horses railed here from Kentucky."

"I'd better clean up before Pepper sees me like this."

"Too late. Looks like her and Odessa headed this way." Stack pointed to the east.

Tap tried to brush the dirt off his torn wool vest as the buck-board rumbled up and parked. Pepper peered out from a well-rounded blanket and smiled at Lowery.

"Stack!"

"Miss Pepper!" Stack beamed. "You're lookin' very, very motherly! It wears good on you."

"Sounds like Tap has warned you what to say. Well, it's won-derful that you could make it!"

"You girls are family. You knew I'd be here."

"I'm sure Selena was counting on it."

"Odessa, you better take good care of my girl," Lowery admonished.

"If I don't bust another leg or have to wear Andrews's Sunday suit again, I think I can take care of her just fine." Lorenzo grinned.

"Speaking of Mr. Andrews," Pepper added. "I suppose that dirt-and-blood-covered object with the silly, toothy grin is my husband."

"Eh . . . sorry, darlin'. There was a little trouble. But it's okay now." Tap shrugged.

"What does the other man look like?" she asked.

"Other men," Stack corrected her. "Two of 'em laid flat in the barn."

"Are they dead?" she asked.

"Nope. Just knocked silly," Stack reported.

"Well . . . he's getting better. Can we get on with this wedding so I can take my husband home and keep him out of trouble?"

"Shall we all meet at the courthouse?" Odessa asked.

"Yep. How about you usin' this rig to go pick up Miss Selena?" Stack nodded toward the fancy carriage. "After Andrews scrubs up in the stock tank, we'll haul him on down and meet you."

Lorenzo Odessa eased himself out of the buckboard and limped over to the carriage. "Thanks, Stack. This is a beautiful setup. I'm obliged to you for lettin' us borrow it."

"I didn't say you could borrow it."

"What?" Odessa shoved back his hat and rubbed his forehead.

"This is my weddin' present."

"It's what?" Odessa gasped.

"It's sort of a dowry for Miss Selena."

"You're joshin' me!"

Stack Lowery put his hands on his hips. "Why would I do that?"

"You can't just give away a carriage like this!" Odessa protested.

"What's the use of owning a gold mine if I can't give things to my friends?"

"Half a gold mine," Tap corrected him.

5

At 1:06 P.M., Saturday, October 6, 1883, in Billings, Montana Territory, Selena Oatley and Lorenzo Odessa repeated solemn vows in front of Judge T. L. Rathdrum in the presence of Mr. Stack Lowery, Miss Angelita Gomez, and Mr. and Mrs. Tapadera Andrews. Mr. Andrews's jacket was mostly clean. The rest of him was a mess.

At 1:35 P.M. Stack Lowery boarded the Northern Pacific westbound. At 1:45 P.M. Mr. and Mrs. Odessa checked into the largest suite at the Gold King Hotel. And at 3:10 P.M. a small procession left Billings going eastward along the Yellowstone River Valley road.

Tap's Colt .44 hung on his hip. Pepper lounged by his side. Tethered behind the grocery-filled buckboard was the big steel-gray gelding, Roundhouse. At the side of the wagon, Angelita straddled Onespot. In her gloved right hand were lead ropes for the yearlings.

"Can I name the ponies?" Angelita called out.

Pepper slipped her hand into the sleeve of Tap's canvas coat. "I can't understand how you could buy two ponies when we have thirty horses at the ranch."

"All we have at the ranch are geldings."

"But you said we're going to buy a stallion and some brood mares."

"That won't be until next spring. These two will be half-grown by then. I was just thinkin' about Lil' Tap."

"Lil' Tap won't need a horse for several years."

"Are you two ignoring me?" Angelita called.

"He'll need one when he's two," Tap announced.

"Two? My son is not getting on a big horse when he's two!"

Tap glanced at her without a smile. "Mine is."

"I'm talking to you!" Angelita hollered again.

"But," Pepper continued, "that doesn't explain why we needed *two* ponies."

"I told you the filly's for Lil' Tapina."

"There's no way in the world my daughter's climbing on a horse at age two."

"Mine is." Tap stared straight ahead as Pepper slipped her hand out of his arm.

"Ahem! Would you two quit fighting and pay attention to me."

"We're not fighting," Tap insisted.

"Of course we are," Pepper countered.

"We are not!"

"Yes, we are."

"Look," Angelita barked, "if you two don't straighten up, I'll send you to your room without supper the minute we get home."

Tap glanced at Pepper, and they both broke into smiles. "Okay, Lil' Mama, we'll quit arguin'."

"Fighting," Pepper corrected.

"That's it." Angelita sighed. "I don't know what I'm going to do with you two. It's beyond me why you think you're ready to embark on the lifelong challenge of parenthood."

Tap turned to Pepper. "Where does she come up with lines like that?"

"She reads too much."

Angelita announced, "I've named the ponies Albert and Victoria."

Tap looked up with a blank expression. "Which is which?"

"Very funny! What do you think? Can we name them that? Please!"

"Well, I don't know, lil' darlin'. Queen Vic isn't exactly the quiet, shy type like that filly, and Prince Albert is dead."

"What difference does that make?" Angelita quizzed.

"Sounds good to me," Pepper commented.

Tap studied the two ponies. "If it's understood that Lil' Tap and Lil' Tapina can rename them if they want to."

"He's extremely confident that you will want to have more than one child," Angelita observed.

"At the moment he's a very optimistic man."

Tap turned to look into Pepper's green eyes. "How are you feeling, darlin'?"

"Every square inch of my body is bloated and puffy. My lower back has a throbbing pain that hasn't let up in three weeks. My tailbone feels like I was dropped off a tower and landed on Plymouth Rock. For no apparent reason, I break out in a sweat like a pig on a spit over a fire. My ankles are so swollen I can no longer tie my shoes—which I can't reach nor see anyway. By noon most days my knees ache, and I get winded walking across the front room. Yesterday I was in the privy and was afraid I couldn't stand up without help. . . . Shall I go on? Or were you expecting me to say, 'Oh, I'm fine'?"

Tap glanced at Angelita. "See what you have to look forward to?"

"Not me. I'm not having children. They can be such a bother. You know what I mean?"

"Well, cowboy, now that I've given you a report," Pepper said as she reached up to rub the back of Tap's neck, "how are *you* feeling?"

"Well," he began, "my left arm feels like someone laid a hot poker against it. My shins have foot-long bruises and seem to give out on me ever' once in a while. I'm still picking gravel out of my hair, and my neck locks up ever' time I have to turn it to the right in a hurry."

"Yes, but are you hurt?" Pepper laid her head on his shoulder.

"Oh, no. This is nothin'. In the old days, if I didn't wake up on Monday feelin' like this, I'd consider the weekend a waste of time."

"What are we going to do with you, Tapadera Andrews?"

"Me?"

"Yes," Angelita called out. "It's obvious you cannot stay out of trouble for five minutes when left on your own. I really shouldn't have stayed with Miss Selena."

"I'll tell you what. Why don't I stay on the ranch from now on, and we'll send someone else to town."

"That would be a start," Pepper agreed. "Let's see . . . We make sure someone goes with you when you ride out on the ranch. . . . You can't ride off Slash-Bar-4 property. . . . You can't wander around the yard unless I can see you from the front window. . . ."

"And he's not allowed to answer the front door," Angelita concluded.

"You're hopeless, Andrews." Pepper brushed strands of blonde hair back off her ears. "I guess we'll just have to trust the Lord to take care of you."

"I reckon that's what He had in mind all along." Tap slapped the reins. The team quickened their pace to a trot.

Tap Andrews had watched the fast-moving clouds pile up in the east all afternoon. They felt a sprinkle or two when they stopped at sundown and cooked some supper along the trail. They hadn't seen another traveler since they turned north on Bull Mountain Road.

Darkness crept in before they reached the western edge of the ranch. Angelita now rode, blanket-covered, next to Pepper. Roundhouse and Onespot trailed the wagon. The young horses' lead ropes were tied to Angelita's side of the wagon. With a heavy, threatening cloud cover, Tap could hardly see the trail. But far up on the mountain, lights glowed through the night.

"Looks like someone's waitin' for us," he commented.

"Is this man Renten trustworthy?" Pepper asked.

"He'll use his last bullet to defend you."

"He mentioned helping you and Odessa escape from a Mexican jail."

Tap laughed. "He told you about that?"

"No. He just mentioned that it happened. You never told me about it."

"Nope."

"Do you want to tell me now?" she prodded.

"Nope."

"Is some young lady's brother going to come searching for you to avenge his sister's honor?"

"Nope. She didn't have any brothers." He looked over at Angelita. "How's little sis?"

"Asleep."

"How's Lil' Tap?"

"Asleep, apparently."

"Well, why don't you join them? It'll be an hour before we reach those lights."

"I want to watch them. It helps me know what others see when they ride up to our place. It's an impressive ranch."

"It's big. I surely hope I know what I'm doin'."

Pepper pulled the wool blanket up to her neck. "Do you think it will rain before we get there?"

"Smells like it."

"What are you planning on doing the next few days?"

"I won't hardly be out of sight. I'll hang around headquarters until you're sick of me and want me to ride off."

"Did you get hit in the head?" she asked.

"A time or two. Why?"

"Because you're starting to sound delirious."

A shaved and scrubbed Howdy Renten held a brass kerosene lantern at the front gate for them. Tap drove the wagon through and then waited for Renten to close it behind them. "You look all dandied up," Tap called out.

Howdy held the lantern high above his head. "You don't. Did you bring me any tobacco?"

"It's back there in the grocery crates."

"You get Odessa married off?"

"Yep. He and Mrs. Odessa should be comin' home tomorrow."

"Tapadera Andrews and Lorenzo Odessa both married. I never figured I'd see that day."

"You didn't think we were the marryin' kind?"

Renten grabbed the harness of the lead horse and led it up to the front of the house. "Shoot, I didn't reckon either of ya would live long enough to git married." Howdy held out his free hand to help Angelita and Pepper down. "Mrs. Andrews, did you ever—"

"Please call me Pepper."

"No, ma'am, I cain't do that. Boss lady is always Missus. Rules of the range."

"In a society where most men can neither read nor write, there seem to be a lot of rules."

"Yes, ma'am, I reckon there are. As I was sayin', did you ever know ol' Tap here when he wasn't injured from a fight?"

"No, I haven't."

"Me neither. Do you reckon he enjoys pain?"

"All right, you two," Tap interrupted. "We've got a wagon to unload, ponies to corral—"

"You find them two orphans wanderin' in the wilderness?" Renten asked.

"No. Bought 'em from a traveling salesman."

"He was selling ponies?"

While Howdy grabbed a box of supplies from the back of the wagon, Tap helped Pepper up the stairs to the porch. Her legs felt heavy and stiff. "Actually," Tap replied, "he was selling Female Remedy."

"He was selling what?" Pepper gasped.

"Female Remedy."

"And you didn't buy me any?" She jabbed an elbow into his side.

"It's too late for you, Mama," Angelita giggled as she scampered ahead of them into the house.

"Mrs. Andrews, there's some supper waitin' on top of the stove and a pie in the warmin' oven."

"Mr. Renten, I'm grateful for your work."

"It's my job, ma'am. Now you and little Miss—eh, Miss—"

"Howdy, this is Angelita Gomez, our house guest. Just treat her like our daughter," Tap instructed.

"Well, you two beautiful ladies go on into the house. Me and Tap will tote them groceries."

"I can't believe you have a pie waiting for us!" Pepper exclaimed as she entered the front room.

"Oh, well . . . I didn't bake the pie. Mrs. Miller did."

"The Quaker lady?" Tap entered the house behind them, carrying a crate of supplies. "She sent a pie all the way to our house?"

"Sent—nothin'! The whole family is camped out at the bunkhouse."

Tap stopped in the middle of the room. "The whole family came to visit?"

"Ain't no social call. Some hombres burned their house and barn and chased off their stock. I'm not sure how many kids they have, but that oldest boy helped me look after the horses."

"How old is he?" Angelita asked.

"About your age, I reckon."

"Maybe I should go and—"

"Stay put, young lady!" Tap thundered. Then he turned back to Howdy. "You figure they're still awake?"

"They turned the lights out a couple hours back," Renten answered.

"Then we'll talk to them in the mornin'. Darlin', I'll put the team up and tuck Albert and Queen Vic into their new home."

"Queenie!" Angelita called out. "I like that even better than Victoria. Let's call her Queenie."

"Then Queenie it is. You and Mama go get yourself some supper and get ready for bed. I'll be back in a few minutes."

Tap was in the barn right after daybreak when Ezra Miller found him. "Brother Andrews, I must apologize for moving into your bunkhouse uninvited last evening. Your hired man assured me it would be all right, but I should have waited and asked you directly. It's just that Mrs. Miller and the children were upset, and at that time of the evening I didn't know what else to do."

Tap scooped oats into a bucket. "Ezra, you and your family are welcome here. No apology is needed. Are any of them hurt?"

"No, we escaped unharmed. But they did their best to frighten us."

"What happened?"

Ezra Miller followed Tap from stall to stall. "They came back the next night and rode right up to the barn—set it on fire and scattered the stock. Peter—that's my eldest—and I tried to stop them, but they wouldn't listen to reason."

"Reason?" Tap shook the oat bucket in front of Onespot. "They only listen to the roar of a shotgun or a .44-40."

"We don't believe in violence, Brother Andrews."

"Don't you think the Lord wants you to protect your family?"

"My family is safe. They are all here with me." Miller unbuttoned the sleeves of his wool shirt and rolled them up. "The Almighty be praised."

Tap stared at the bushy eyebrows and beard of the broad-shouldered man. *Lord, I don't understand this way of thinkin'.* "How did you make it to the ranch?"

"The only stock they left us were the draft horses. So at day-break we hooked up the wagon and came looking for your ranch."

"Were you able to save your belongings?" Tap asked.

"You mean, bring them with us?"

"Yep. Could you salvage your personal things?"

"Oh, we only brought a few things. Peter and I will go back today and round up the stock. Then we'll rebuild the house. Actually, only the canvas and some of the furnishings burned. We'll cut more timbers and finish the house."

Tap grabbed a pitchfork to muck a stall. "You're goin' to move back?"

"It's our farm. I've got the papers. I'm not the type to just walk away." Miller pulled a rake from the wall and began to help Andrews.

"Ezra, this is wild country out here. I was born and raised here. It's all I know. I've learned that you can stop good men with reason but bad men only with force—and violent men with a .44-40." Even though it was a cool morning, Tap sweated through his cotton shirt. He pulled off his canvas jacket.

"God will provide for us," Miller assured him.

"Well . . ." Tap grabbed the handles of the wheelbarrow and shoved it out the open barn door. "A man's got to follow how the Lord's leadin' him. I've learned that much. I guess He sort of leads different people in different ways. Whenever you're ready to ride back, I'll saddle up and go with you. I'll help gather your stock."

"Thank you, Brother Andrews. . . . Mrs. Miller was right. She said you would offer to go with us. But I can't ask you to do that. It's a long trip. We might be gone for several days. You have family responsibilities here."

"Things are startin' to settle down." Tap dumped the load and returned to the barn. He led Roundhouse to one of the horse corrals. Miller tagged along behind him. "Mr. Odessa and his wife will be back to the ranch today or tomorrow. And Howdy is here, so I can take a day or two to help out a neighbor."

Miller chewed a piece of straw and waved his strong, callused hand. "Brother Andrews, if I might be so blunt—I don't want to accept your help. I have to know if I can take care of my family on my own. If my peace and success is based on the firearms of friendly neighbors, then . . . then I might as well take up a violent life myself. I've got to prove to myself I can handle this. Do you understand?"

Tap rubbed his neck. He could feel his icy cold fingers and the stubble of a one-day beard. "I reckon I do," he replied. "You're about as stubborn as I am."

"It's my stubbornness that brought us here. Mrs. Miller wanted us to settle with a colony of Friends in Nebraska, but I insisted we push on and find a better land. If I had listened to her, we would all be safe, I suppose."

"Well, safety isn't the highest of virtues," Tap offered.

"Now that, Brother Andrews, is something we completely agree upon."

"So what can I do to help?"

"Your hospitality for my wife and younger children is an unrepayable debt. If they might stay in your bunkhouse until Peter and I return, you will be a blessing from heaven."

"Miller, I haven't often been called a blessin' from heaven. It goes without sayin' they can stay. You got enough room? The cows got in there the other day. I tried to clean it up."

"It's a very large room. Each child had a bed last night. They think it's a mansion."

"What time will you be pulling out?"

"Within the hour."

"Take a grub bag with you. Howdy can help you out."

"We have supplies at the farm."

"They might have burned those up too."

"Why would they do that?" Miller asked.

Tap just shook his head and sauntered back into the barn to get Onespot.

Ezra Miller and his son Peter were hitching their team to the farm wagon when Angelita ran out. Tap was in a corral examining a swollen leg on one of the horses in the roundup string. She wore a long off-white dress, black high-top lace-up shoes, and two pigtails that hung down her back to her waist.

"Mr. Renten brought us over some breakfast. Mama said to call you in."

Tap climbed the four-rail cedar fence and jumped down next to Angelita. "You ladies feelin' rested after that big day yesterday?"

"I'm sure I look very cute today, but I do feel tired. How's your arm?" Her words were directed to Tap, but her eyes searched the yard, especially the Miller wagon.

"It's ugly and it hurts. Pepper must have poured half a bottle of iodine on it last night."

"I know." Angelita's voice came out almost like she was singing. "I heard you scream."

"I didn't scream."

"You hollered."

"I might have grimaced a little, but that's all."

"You grimaced very, very loudly!" Angelita skipped on ahead of Tap and stopped near the Miller wagon.

"Hello, I'm Angelita Gomez. I'm staying with Mr. and Mrs. Andrews. Actually they treat me like I was their daughter."

Tap trailed along behind her. "Eh . . . Angelita," Tap began, "this is Mr. Miller."

She looked back at Tap and rolled her brown eyes to the sky in disgust.

"Oh . . . yes, and I believe this young man is named Peter," Tap added.

Angelita curtsied as Peter Miller blushed and tried to look busy with the rigging of the wheel horse. "Are you twelve years old?" she demanded.

"Me?" Peter gasped.

"You certainly didn't think I was addressing your father, did you?" Her eyes were steadily fixed on his.

"Oh . . . yeah . . . I'm twelve—almost thirteen," he asserted, looking down at his worn brown boots.

"Well, I'll be twelve next year, although I look older. But if you're going to live around here, there is something you need to know. The man I marry has to own a gold mine."

"Uh . . . what?" Peter Miller choked.

"I'm sure you're disappointed, but I think it's important to be honest right from the start." Angelita took off on a run to the big house, leaving Ezra Miller and Tap to stare at each other. Peter Miller's mouth hung half open.

Tap swallowed hard. "Eh . . . she's not exactly the bashful type."

Pepper and Angelita sat at the big oak table when Tap entered the dining room wiping his wet hands on a flour sack towel.

"Look at this!" Pepper spread her arms across the food on the table.

"Howdy?"

"He delivered it all in a basket. I feel guilty," Pepper admitted.

"How guilty?" Tap prodded.

"Not too guilty." She flashed him that dimpled smile that always reminded Tap why she was the queen of every dance hall she ever worked in. She broke open a raised flour biscuit. "I heard you and Angelita visited with the Quaker family."

"Eh . . . sort of." Tap scooted into a chair across from them. "Mama, you need to talk to little sis here. That poor Miller boy almost blushed himself to death."

With blonde hair hanging past her shoulders and still clothed in her gray wool robe, Pepper scowled at Angelita. "What did you do to him?"

Angelita folded a strip of thick bacon, wedged it into her biscuit, and then crammed it into her mouth. "He umphh, nat massful."

"What did you say?" Pepper asked, holding an egg-laden fork in her hand.

Angelita swallowed hard. "He's too bashful. Obviously he hasn't spent much time around beautiful women."

As they ate breakfast, Tap relayed the conversation he had had earlier with Ezra Miller. He was finishing a second cup of coffee when Angelita pushed back from the table and packed the dishes out to the kitchen.

"Mama, when are you and I going to visit the Millers?" she called back.

"Peter's going with his father back to their farm," Tap informed her.

"I know that. I wanted to meet all his family."

Tap had Roundhouse saddled and bucked out when Howdy Renten wandered out of the cook shack and over to the corrals. "It's goin' to rain before the day's out," he announced. "Better take your fish."

Tap gazed up at the clouds loosely stacked above the brown-grassed hills. "You might be right. I've got my slicker tied on the cantle."

"You and Odessa plannin' on takin' care of them cows all winter by yourself?"

"We might pick up a hand or two, but I'm in no hurry. When we bring up the rest of the stock in the spring, we'll need a full crew."

"You want me to ride out with you today?"

"No, I need you here. We've got a hacienda full of women and kids. I need someone to keep the wolves away."

"Two-legged or four-legged?"

"Both."

Howdy rubbed his face. "I feel nakid as a baby without a

beard. I should've never shaved. Don't know what got into me. A bath and a shave, and it's only September."

"October."

"Whatever." Renten brushed his teeth with his finger and then spat. "You want me to feed the horses?"

"I did that this morning, but I would like you to rearrange the barn to make room for Selena's deluxe new carriage."

"You really expect them back today?"

"Yep."

"How come?"

"'Cause I only paid for that fancy room for one night. Did you ever know Lorenzo to have more than ten dollars in his pocket?"

"Ten? I never knowed him to have more than two."

Tap cinched his saddle down a little tighter and then walked around and mounted Roundhouse from the right side.

"You ridin' an Indian pony?" Howdy queried.

"That's what I surmise." Tap spun Roundhouse to the right until he settled down. "I'm headed east to the edge of the ranch, then up to the tree line, and back to the ranch. Should be home by early afternoon. I want to see how far I can let them drift in a storm without gettin' into trouble."

"You goin' to ride up and check on the Quaker and his son?"

"Nope. It's too far away, plus he doesn't want my help. Told me so himself. I respect that."

"Well . . . this is pretty tough country to just turn the other cheek."

Tap pulled his black hat down and slid the keeper on his horse-hair stampede string tight under his chin. "Each man finds his own callin', I guess, Howdy. Providin' it's the same God callin'."

The squeak of saddle leather sounded good to Tap's ears after a day of riding bent-legged in the buckboard. He stretched his long legs in the stirrups and trotted Roundhouse to the east. Most of the 500 head were scattered between the headquarters and the river. The grass was buckskin-brown but thick. Tap figured it hadn't been grazed for almost two years.

He and Roundhouse meandered through the cattle. Both man and horse seemed to be memorizing both ends of each longhorn. Coming to the edge of the grazing herd, he hazed a few stragglers back to the west and then spurred the gray gelding east. Tap figured he was about four or five miles from the Yellowstone River. He rode parallel with the river, about halfway between it and the Bull Mountains. He couldn't see a tree, a building, or an animal between the river and the mountains, except for Castle Butte, standing like a rocky pimple on the brown face of the sloping prairie. The wind was at his back, and the clouds had bunched up tighter than earlier in the day.

This is what I love, Lord. Ridin' for miles on our place and never seeing a soul. Pepper's right. I get along better without many folks around. Just me and a good horse, some cows, and a good woman . . . a beautiful, good woman . . . a beautiful, good woman who's expecting. Except, Lord, she's miserable, and I can't do a thing about it.

Even though the clouds blocked the sun, Tap calculated it was a little past noon when he came to a steep gulch that he and Stack had figured several weeks ago was the eastern edge of the ranch. Spying a trail down the side of the coulee, Tap spurred Roundhouse down the sandy path until he came to a dry creekbed.

"Those are fresh tracks, Roundy . . . one Indian pony maybe. At least one that wasn't wearin' shoes. Looks like a busy thoroughfare. They could probably ride up this coulee to the mountains and be hard to spot. The last ones through were headed toward the river."

Tap pulled his .44 Winchester '73 rifle, cocked the lever, and then gently released the hammer down to the safety position and laid it across his lap. He rode south along the creekbed, following the horse tracks. It took him over an hour to reach the mouth, which ended at the top of a rocky bluff overlooking the Northern Pacific rail lines and the Yellowstone River. During the spring runoff, the little creek would make a dramatic waterfall. Across the river were white cliffs that marked the beginning of the Crow Indian Reserve. He was still half a mile from the river. The first thing he spotted was a very long, unpainted wooden building.

"Roundhouse, what do we have down there? This is the crazi-est country. If you put a trail in a coulee and a building in a canyon, no one even knows they're there. I mean, no one but those trav-elin' along the river or the rail. Come on, boy . . . let's go visitin'."

Tap and Roundhouse picked their way back and forth among the boulders until they reached the bottom of the cliff. The trail he followed out of the coulee swung left toward a sand bar reach-ing out into the river. But halfway to the water, a faint trail branched off and led to the building. The brush was thick as they paralleled the river back to the west.

He heard a gunshot inside the building. Cocking the hammer of the rifle back, he walked Roundhouse slowly out into the clear-ing. The building bore only a hand-painted sign: Starke & Cantrell, Goods & Services.

Tap threw his rifle to his shoulder when a man wearing a yel-low sash dove out the doorway, flung himself off the front porch into the dirt, and fired several shots back at the open doorway. Then he crawled under the boardwalk porch.

Andrews yanked back a couple times on the reins. Roundhouse backed up into the brush. A shotgun blast ended the shooting inside the building. Tap waited for movement, but no one ven-tured through the door, nor did the man under the porch try to come out. Instead the man rolled to his back and pointed his revolver straight up through the cracks in the boardwalk.

Tap debated whether to point his rifle toward the open door-way or at the man underneath. *Lord, have mercy on 'em. I don't even know which side, if any, is in the right. There's nothin' I can do but let them play their hand.*

Then a man who looked about thirty, wearing a long-sleeved blue shirt and ducking trousers, stepped to the doorway with a shotgun in his right hand, blood streaming down his left. The man underneath the porch seemed to be waiting for him to take one more step. Suddenly the man with the shotgun glanced down.

Both guns roared at once. The wounded man with the shotgun crumpled to the porch. The man underneath screamed and grabbed his face, then rolled out from under the building, and staggered to his feet. With his face still in his hand, he toppled onto the dirt in front of the store.

Tap waited in the trees, his rifle at his shoulder.

No sound.

No movement.

Nothing.

Finally he shoved his rifle back into the scabbard and dismounted. Tying Roundhouse to a bush, Tap stepped behind a cottonwood tree that had an eight-inch trunk. "Ho, in the store! I'm just a neighbor passin' by. . . . You need any help in there?"

No reply.

"I said, do you need any help? Are you hurt?"

With Colt .44 in hand, Tap inched his way toward the building. The downed man in the yard and the man on the porch weren't breathing. Cautiously peeking inside the store, Tap strained to see through the acrid gun smoke that hung in the air. A man's body sprawled across several packing crates. He was wearing a yellow sash like the one in the yard. *Shot at close range with a shotgun. No need checking for a pulse.*

A wide double door at the middle of the store led to the other end of the building. Tap swung one of the doors open slowly. . . . *A saloon? The sign didn't mention a saloon . . . did it?*

As his eyes adjusted to the dimness of the room, he saw a man sprawled under a worn poker table at the back.

All four died in the shoot-out?

As he approached, he could see the man's chest expand and contract. *This one's still breathing.*

Tap crawled under the table and gently turned the man over. "Where are you shot, mister?" he asked.

The man remained unconscious.

"Mister, I don't see any bullet hole in you! I don't see any blue lump on your head. You either fainted or passed out. From the way you smell, I'd say you're drunk."

Tap stepped behind the rough-cut wooden bar and grabbed up a blue enameled tin washbasin full of grimy water. Still holding his revolver with his right hand, he tossed the dirty water on the man's face. With wild red eyes and a startled expression, the man sat straight up, slamming his head into the frame of the solid oak table. He immediately collapsed back to the floor. His worn modest dark blue suit, white shirt, and tie all looked as if they had been slept in for a month.

Tap's boot toe prodded the man's ribs.

"Come on, mister, there's been a little trouble here. Maybe you can help me sort it out."

The man opened his left bloodshot eye and squinted at Tap. "I ain't workin' today. This is my day off. Go see Cantrell."

"You work here?"

With both eyes closed, he continued the conversation. "I told you this is my day off. Let me be. I'm enjoying the fruit of my labor."

"Do you know Starke and Cantrell?"

"Yep."

"Can you identify them? I think they might be dead."

"They ain't."

"How do you know?"

"I'm Horatio Starke. I ain't dead."

The click of Andrews's gun cocked next to the man's head brought both eyes wide open. "Listen, Starke," Andrews growled, "there are three men dead out here, and I think you ought to take a look at them. Business is going to be mighty slow until you bury the bodies."

Starke crawled out from under the table and struggled to his feet. "Dead? You mean . . . dead . . . dead?"

"Yep."

"I need a drink."

"You need a bath. Now get out there and identify the bodies."

Starke stumbled through the door into the store side of the building and gazed at the body on the crates. He raised his hands. "Don't kill me, mister. You kin have the money! It's in a tin under the counter!" he shouted.

"I didn't shoot this man. I think your partner might have. I'm just a neighbor passing by who heard some gunshots."

"You ain't one of them yellow sashes?" He pointed at the dead man.

"Nope."

"Eh . . . well, I was joshin' about the money. There ain't any over there in that tin."

Tap prodded the man with the barrel of his Colt. "Go out on the porch. There's a couple more out there." He shoved his gun in his holster and followed the man out.

"That's Cantrell." Starke pointed to the man wearing the blue shirt, still gripping the shotgun. "We own this place. Well . . . I guess he ain't my partner no more."

Tap reached down and searched for a pulse. He knew it was a waste of time. "How about the other one?" He pointed to the yard.

Starke tottered over to the man in the dirt yard. He kicked the body over with his stocking-clad foot. "He ain't got no face left!"

"Kind of hard to recognize, I expect—"

"I think I'm goin' to puke," Starke gagged.

"You need help with these bodies?" Tap asked.

"Help?"

"You're not going to leave them to rot in your yard, are you?"

"Eh . . . no . . . I need a—a—"

"A shovel?"

"A drink." Starke turned toward the store.

"What about these men?"

"Don't matter. I'm a dead man anyway."

"How do you figure?" Tap pressed.

"Them two are in the Yellow Sash gang. They find out these two was shot dead here at the store, they'll come after me. Cantrell should've given them the money."

"Yellow Sash bunch?"

"You ain't never heard of the Yellow Sash gang? You must be new around here."

"I'm runnin' the Slash-Bar-4."

"May the Lord have mercy on your soul. They'll probably be after you next."

"What about this gang?"

"Ever'one of them's mean, and ever'one will shoot you in the back if you ain't lookin'."

"No one's been able to catch them?"

"Lots have tried. They either come back empty—or dead."

"How long have they been gettin' away with this?"

"They moved into this country with the railroad. They followed the lines—stealin', cheatin', bushwhackin' workers out of their pay. When the line was completed, they settled in the hills down on the Crow Reserve and come raidin' up here whenever they get short on supplies. Some say them Crows is in cahoots with 'em. Somethin's got to be done. They got $4,000 off the Northern Pacific last month. We figured we wouldn't see 'em 'til spring."

"You were wrong."

"Dead wrong." Starke paused by the body of his partner on the front steps and then turned back to Tap. "Mister, you ain't interested in buyin' this place, are you? I'll give you a real bargain."

"Nope."

"The N. P. might put in a tie sidin' by March, and if they do, we'll have more business than we know what to do with. Sure you don't want to buy me out?"

"Not me."

"Well." Starke shrugged. "I guess I better notify his kin. Told me he had a sister, Miss Carolina Cantrell, back east. Maybe she wants to buy the place."

Tap gazed around. *An Eastern lady runnin' this dump?*

"You want to come have a drink with me?"

"I don't drink."

"You ain't another one of them Quakers, is ya? Nah, I guess not. You're packin' a sidearm. Well, I'm goin' to have a drink."

"And you can take care of these bodies. I'm goin' back to the ranch. If the sheriff wants to get my story, send him out to the Slash-Bar-4."

Starke was completely out of sight by the time Tap finished his sentence. He hiked out to Roundhouse, mounted up, rode out three quick bucks, and headed back up to the grassland slope.

Angelita led a parade of children to the front porch of the big house, and Pepper stepped outside to survey the crew.

"This is Ellen Mae." Angelita introduced the tallest of the

Miller children. "She's eleven and knows how to make quilts."
She moved down the row to the next tallest, a dark-haired boy
with black trousers and a long-sleeved white shirt. "And this is
Chester Leroy. He's nine and—"

"I'm almost ten."

"He's nine," Angelita repeated. "He claims he can stand on his
hands and walk clear across the yard."

"I can. Do you want to see me?"

"Oh, not right now, Chester Leroy." Pepper smiled.

"Everybody calls me Chet—except for her." He pointed at
Angelita.

"This is Margaret Louise. She's seven."

"I'm six, and I can cook an apple pie."

"Well . . ." Angelita looked at the round brown eyes of the little girl, whose face was set off by two long braids of sandy-blonde
hair. "She looks mature for her age, don't you think?"

"Is that good?" Margaret Louise asked.

"Yes. Now this is Ruth Raylene. She's three."

A little round face with shoulder-length dark hair peeked out
from under a knit hat. Her coat was only buttoned at the top, and
the sleeves hung well over her hands. She held out three chubby
fingers. "I can count to ten!" she squealed.

"The baby's name is Matthew Mark, and he's eighteen months
old. He's not here because he's . . . busy eating his dinner."

"Mother said she would come pay her respects when she finished with Matthew Mark," Ellen Mae reported.

"There's one more. His name is Peter James Miller, and he's
almost thirteen. He went with his father to try to round up the
stock. He has dark brown hair, straight teeth, brown eyes, strong
shoulders, dimples when he smiles, and he blushes very easily. But
he doesn't have a gold mine."

"Well," Pepper laughed, "I think I'd like to meet him anyway."

"This is Mama." Angelita pointed to Pepper. "She's not really
this big all the time. She's great with child. And she knows everything—except how to play the piano. We used to have a big piano
that she couldn't play in our home in Cheyenne, but they burned
down our house."

"They burned up our house too," Ellen Mae reported. "But my daddy's going to build it back."

"May we play on the porch, Mama?" Angelita asked.

"Yes, certainly. What are you going to play?"

Angelita took a deep breath and sighed. "We're going to play school. I get to be the teacher, of course."

"Naturally," Pepper replied. "I think I'll go for a walk. I need some fresh air."

"Where will you go?" Angelita asked.

"Just out to the gate and over to the barn to look at the ponies. "How are Queenie and Albert doing today?"

"Albert is very friendly, but Queenie is more bashful than some almost-thirteen-year-old boys I know," Angelita replied.

After Pepper had circled the headquarters and checked on the yearlings, she swung around by the bunkhouse. A dark-haired woman, not much older than herself, stepped out on the porch carrying a baby in a blanket.

"Mrs. Andrews?"

"Mrs. Miller."

"I can't tell you how much we appreciate you allowing us to use the bunkhouse."

"I'm glad we can be neighborly." Pepper stepped closer to the porch of the bunkhouse. "Tap and I figure it's one of the reasons the Lord allowed us to have this place."

"Mr. Andrews is a believer, is he?"

"Yes, but it's a struggle for both of us. We weren't raised in the faith, and it's still very new."

"It looks like you'll be delivering in a week or two," Mrs. Miller noted.

"The doctor in Pine Bluffs assured me it would be the first of November. But I'm not sure he's right."

"He's not. Trust me. I know, Mrs. Andrews." Mrs. Miller cuddled the small blanketed face in her arms.

"Please call me Pepper."

"And I'm Lucy." She stepped down off the porch. "How many children do you have?"

"This is my first," Pepper blurted out. "Well, that's not quite right. I lost an earlier child that I carried for eight months. And Angelita is the child of a friend of ours. Her mother died, and her father was crippled by a bullet. We're raising her—at least we're trying. We love her dearly, just like our own, but she can be impetuous at times."

"Well, she's captured the imagination of my whole clan. They follow her around like baby quails after their mother."

Pepper thought she felt a sprinkle of rain hit her face as she glanced at Mrs. Miller's tired eyes. "Come up to the big house after a while, and I'll boil some peppermint tea. We could sit and visit."

"Is Mr. Andrews at home?"

"No. He had to go out and look at the cattle. But even if he's at home, it would be no bother."

"I'd like very much to visit with both of you," Mrs. Miller admitted. "It's been so long since I've had anyone to talk to."

"When Tap comes back, I'll send Angelita over to call you."

"That would be delightful. I really need your advice." Mrs. Miller sighed.

6

Four miles from headquarters the gates of heaven opened, and water thundered to the earth. Each drop of rain seemed to be shot out of the sky, hitting the dry Montana sod like a bullet, blasting up a plume of dust. But the raindrops didn't stop. And soon each drop was splashing onto mud.

Tap pulled on his yellow slicker, shoved the stampede string tight against his neck, and slumped in the saddle to keep the water rolling off his broad shoulders. As he turned north away from the river, the wind picked up, and the rain swept diagonally across the grass prairie incline.

It's a lousy place to be stuck in a storm, Lord. No shelter, no firewood, no cabin, no cave. When the clouds block the mountains, there's not a landmark in sight. If this was blowin' snow, a man could wander around in circles and never find his way back in.

We ought to build a little line shack down here. Just a storm cabin. Put a man in it through the winter. He could keep the cattle from drifting into the river . . . and the bushwhackers from coming up on the ranch. Ought to build another cabin up on Cedar Mesa. I don't want to lose cows in the mountains. With just 500 head though, I won't need to do it this winter. Maybe I'll keep some of the spring branding crew through the summer if they can carpenter.

Even though the top button on his slicker was fastened tight against his neck, Tap could feel a stream of cold rain soak through the collar of his shirt and across his shoulders. His ducking trousers sponged the brisk rain, which dribbled down his legs into his boots.

Well, Pepper darlin', we'll find out if the roof leaks today.

Tap peeked out from under the now-limp wide brim of his beaver felt hat but could not see any sign of the headquarters.

His left arm began to burn along the wound. His wet ducking trousers grated against the insides of his knees as they gripped Roundhouse's flanks. Even with his hat pulled down, the icy rain ran off his ears, nose, and chin. His smooth leather gloves felt as if they weighed five pounds each, as they absorbed the water.

Roundhouse dropped his head down and settled into a fast walk. The storm clouds hung so low and heavy that it seemed as if it were surely suppertime, but Tap knew it couldn't be later than midafternoon.

He cut across the drive leading up to the headquarters and turned the gray gelding north. Even the slosh of the downpour didn't completely obliterate fresh carriage tracks.

Looks like the newlyweds made it home. Don't reckon anyone else would drive a two-horse carriage out here. That's good. If the weather breaks by mornin', Odessa and I can ride along the mountains and build up those boundary markers.

A rivulet of runoff water streamed across the drive as Tap finally reached the twelve-foot-wide, unpainted wood front gate. The big house was on the highest spot, but all the ground sloped to the south in the direction of the Yellowstone River. The only standing water of any consequence that Tap could spot was in the corrals in a low place made by milling animals and by scooping out manure.

Tap walked Roundhouse through the open door of the barn. Howdy Renten was brushing down a big black horse, while another, with feed sack tied around his nose, stood tethered to an iron hitching ring. In the breezeway at the back of the barn stood a new black carriage.

"I think it might rain today!" Howdy called out as he glanced up at the soaked Andrews.

"Won't amount to much, I reckon," Tap replied, unloading from the right side of the saddle.

"Nah . . . a man probably won't even get wet."

Tap pulled the saddle off Roundhouse and slung it and the wool saddle blanket on the partition of an empty stall. "So Mr. and Mrs. Odessa returned home?"

"About an hour ago. Headed straight for the cottage, I surmise," Renten added.

Tap stepped over by the black carriage that had already been wiped clean of mud. "She's a real beauty, isn't she?"

Howdy didn't look up. "That she is. A real beauty. That Odessa is a lucky man."

"I meant the carriage." Tap laughed.

"I thought we was talking about Mrs. Odessa."

"Obviously."

"Do either one of them women know what they're gettin' into, marryin' the likes of you two?"

"Nope."

"Just as well." Howdy spat a wad of tobacco out into the middle of the barn floor. "Say, Odessa did have a message for you."

"What's that?"

"The sheriff was scoutin' around town, mountin' up a posse."

"A posse?"

"Them two old boys you left flat in the livery got themselves patched up enough to go down and rob the River Valley Bank of over $2,000."

"Jackson and Bean? They don't seem like the bank-robbin' kind."

"Well, the sheriff thinks them two might try to ride down and join up with that Yellow Sash bunch. Have you ever heard of them?"

"Just today. Some of them caught lead down at a little siding joint by the river. I heard they're staying on the Crow Reserve. What's that have to do with us?"

"Sheriff says they might swing out on this side of the river to throw 'em off and then cross around at Bull Mountain ferry. He asked us to be on the lookout."

"We won't find many tracks after a rain like this," Tap pointed out.

"You go get out of them wet clothes. I'll rub and grain the big gray."

"He's got a tendency to kick if you get too close to that left side."

"So do I." Howdy winked.

The house felt warm and slightly stuffy as Tap pushed open the front door. He carried his rifle and his saddlebags. Pepper sat on the leather sofa, her feet propped up on a pillow, an open Bible in her lap.

"Well, Mr. Montana Rancher, how's our place look in the rain?"

"Wet." Tap tossed his saddlebags over the back of a straight oak chair and propped his rifle against the wall near the front door. "You got any coffee?"

"On the stove in the kitchen. I'll get it for you."

"Stay right there, darlin'. You look too comfortable to disturb."

"Thanks." Pepper slumped back against the sofa.

Tap returned from the kitchen with two porcelain cups steaming with coffee. "Here you go, darlin'."

"Would you like to sit down?" She patted the cushion next to her.

"Think I'll just stand by the fire and try to dry out."

"This is nice," she murmured as she took a sip.

"The coffee?"

"The coffee, the warm fire, the big house—and especially having you come in from work not having been shot at by train robbers or bushwhacked by rustlers. I'm going to like having a rancher husband. I bet you didn't even fire your gun today."

"Nope. I didn't." *'Course I did have to pull it and point it down at Starke and Cantrell's store.* "Eh, did you see Lorenzo and Selena?" He huddled in front of the crackling fire, sipping his coffee.

Pepper laid down her Bible next to the sewing and ran her fingers through the blonde hair that cascaded across her shoulders and down her back. "No, they didn't come over yet. Angelita said they went straight to the cottage."

Tap pulled off his heavy, dripping wool-lined canvas jacket. "I didn't see any light over there."

"Oh, you know how it is on the second day of marriage."

"If I remember right, you and me got up on the second day and cooked for twenty-five house guests, including Selena."

"But that's not what we wanted to do!"

Tap felt her green eyes tug at him. "Mmmm, glory, lady—you are still one pretty woman."

"I bet you say that to all the ladies great with child."

"No, ma'am, you're the first one. That green velvet dress is one of my favorites. I haven't seen it on you in a long time. I figured it was one of those that didn't fit you anymore."

"It doesn't. It was one that was in Suzanne's wardrobe, remember? Anyway, I was just sick of wearing that same faded brown one."

"But how did you . . ."

"I didn't button it in the back. As long as I lean back against the sofa, it works fine."

Tap turned away from the fire to warm his backside. Steam rose off his trousers, vest, and shirt. "Maybe I better put on something dry. Where's Angelita?"

"Correcting papers in her room."

"Doing what?"

"She and several of the Miller children played school on the front porch all day until it began to rain. She borrowed six pieces of paper from your office."

"And she was the teacher?"

"Can you imagine her as anything else?"

"Nope."

"Listen." Pepper took a sip of coffee, held it a moment in her mouth, and then gulped it down. "Mrs. Miller—her name is Lucinda, but she asked that I call her Lucy—wanted to speak to both of us."

"Is there trouble? Did she hear from Mr. Miller?"

"No, I don't think so . . . yet. She just needs someone to talk to."

"I'll go change." He stopped at the doorway. "You know, darlin', I've made a lot of rides in stormy weather. I generally don't like them at all. But this time, knowin' you were here on the ranch waitin' for me made it all sort of seem worthwhile."

"We're home, Mr. Andrews. We're home."

In the history of Pepper Andrews's smiles, Tap considered the one she wore now as one of the two or three best of all times. "My, oh my, you do look pretty."

"You tryin' to sweet-talk me, cowboy?"

"No . . . I mean, it's just . . . your hair combed down, that green dress, the beautiful smile."

"Now there is one needy, desperate husband."

"It shows, huh?"

"It's been a long pregnancy for all of us. But even if you drawled, 'Ah, shucks, Miss Pepper,' I still won't dance with you, drifter."

"Just a few more weeks, darlin', and it's all over."

"Over? Over!" she snapped. The sparkle went right out of her green eyes. "Don't be naive! A few more weeks and it's just beginning!"

"What's beginning?" Angelita interjected as she bounced down the stairs.

"Oh, nothin', lil' darlin'," Tap called. "Mama's just a bit testy." He disappeared into the kitchen.

"Angelita," Pepper instructed, "you get your coat and hat, take the umbrella, and go tell Mrs. Miller that Tap's home. Why don't you offer to stay there with the children so she can visit, and they won't all have to be out in the rain?"

"Oh, good. Maybe I'll go visit Selena and Mr. Odessa too."

"Don't you dare! You leave them alone," Pepper insisted. "We'll know they want company when they come to see us."

"It's only a small cottage. It must be quite boring in there," Angelita huffed. "I'm sure they would appreciate a visit."

Pepper raised her voice. "You may not leave this house, young lady, until you promise me you will not disturb the Odessas!"

"I promise."

"Good. Because I expect you to do exactly what I told you to."

"You know what I think?" Angelita pulled her long wool coat off a peg. "I think we will all be very, very glad when the baby gets here. Maybe you won't be so grouchy then." She pulled her hat down over her ears and stepped out onto the covered porch carrying the umbrella.

Pepper picked up her sewing and stabbed the cloth with a needle. *I certainly am not grouchy! I don't know why everyone says I'm testy when I'm merely expressing legitimate concerns. Perhaps I'm a little too forceful or brusque, but not grouchy. They have no idea what real grouchiness is like. I ought to let them see it, and then they wouldn't be so sensitive about the way I act now. If they were stuck in this body for ten minutes, they'd probably go running out of the house stark, raving mad and throw themselves in the mud!*

Lord, I am not grouchy.

Am I?

Tap shuffled down the stairs wearing a freshly pressed boiled white collarless shirt, clean tan duckings, and black leather suspenders. He carried his stove-top black boots in his hand. "You want another cup of coffee?" he asked her.

"No," she steamed, "I don't want any more coffee!" *Okay, so maybe I am a little grouchy.*

Tap sat on the brick hearth pulling on clean socks.

"Honey, I'm sorry for being so short with everyone today. I must sound horrible. But you married me for 'better or for worse,' right?"

He jerked on his boot and glanced over at her. "Which is this?" He winked.

Pepper stuck out her tongue at him and then broke into a wide grin.

"Oh, my, darlin', that dimpled smile of yours stills puts a lump in my throat and a leap in my heart."

"Good." She patted her protruding stomach. "I'm glad something still works."

Tap stood and walked toward her. "You want me to rub your back?"

A soft, steady knock at the door caused them both to turn and look.

"I want you to open the door," she sighed. "It must be Mrs. Miller."

Lucinda Miller entered the big house wearing a black hooded cape that covered her long navy dress. Tap stepped over. "Let me hang your coat by the fire," he offered. "Please come in and sit down. Can I get you ladies some coffee?"

"That would be delightful, dear," Pepper hummed. "Lucy, please excuse me for not standing."

"I am one person you do not need to explain things to," Mrs. Miller replied. "I'm amazed you're able to fit into such a beautiful dress."

"That's why I can't get up," Pepper whispered. "I didn't button it."

"I have a green measuring dress that's very similar," Lucinda Miller admitted.

"Measuring dress?"

"Yes, after every child is born, I pull out that same dress and keep trying it on until it fits again. That way I know I'm back where I started from. I call it my measuring dress."

Tap came back carrying two cups of coffee. He sat down on the brick hearth and faced the sofa where both women sat. "Now Pepper said you wanted to talk to us. What can we do for you?"

"First, let me repeat what I told Mrs. Andrews. Having you at this ranch has been a godsend for us. We didn't have the cash for a hotel room, even if we could have traveled that far. It's such a pleasant, happy atmosphere here. After one day the children already say it's the most enjoyable place they have ever stayed."

"I'm afraid the bunkhouse isn't all it could be," Tap apologized.

"It's much more accommodating than a hole in the ground, Mr. Andrews. You saw what our place was like."

"Well," he conceded, "sometimes you have to go through some tough times to get the place you want."

"We have to go through tough times just to live until the next day," she replied. Tap watched as she took a deep breath and let it out slowly. Her beige-gloved interlaced hands quivered a little. "I don't know quite where to begin." She stared at the floor. "But

I must talk to someone. May God forgive me if I shouldn't be saying these things."

"Whatever you tell us will be held in strict confidence," Pepper assured her.

Lucinda Miller nodded her head. "I married Ezra when I was fifteen. He was twenty-nine and had spent his entire life in the Quaker faith. This is all new to me, but I loved him dearly and was willing to accept the lifestyle. I mean, I still love my husband dearly. I didn't mean for it to sound otherwise."

"Yes, of course." Pepper nodded.

"Well, in our fifteen years of marriage, we have never lived in the same place more than a year or so. Ezra keeps finding someplace farther west that excites his interest. From Ohio to Indiana to Iowa to Minnesota to Nebraska to Montana—we've scooted along."

"Yes . . . well, this is our fourth home, and we haven't been married a year," Pepper admitted.

"But we intend on being here a long, long time," Tap added.

Mrs. Miller took another deep breath. "Well, all of this wears on me and the children, but I know it also wears on Ezra. He's ready to stop moving. He believes with all his heart that our farm here in Montana is God-given and if we don't stay here, we will be violating divine Providence."

"It's a pretty place," Tap encouraged her.

"It's wonderful," Mrs. Miller acknowledged. "But . . . for reasons unknown to us, violent men want us to leave."

"And you're frightened?" Pepper supplied.

"The thought of perishing does not frighten me, Mrs. Andrews. My confidence is in my Lord and Savior and the place He is preparing for me. But I'm frightened to think my children might have to grow up without a mother—or without a father. I could not run that farm without Ezra, and yet he continually puts himself in a position to be mortally wounded."

"What would you like to happen?" Pepper asked.

"I would like either to move . . . perhaps back to the States where we could be around others of our persuasion. Someplace less violent."

"You said either. What's the other possibility?" Tap questioned.

Mrs. Miller twisted her interlaced fingers and looked away from Tap. "I wish Ezra would point a shotgun at the next bushwhacker who rides into our place and blow him all the way to Hades." She stared over at Tap. "May God forgive me for that thought. I am weak in the faith, Mr. and Mrs. Andrews. I have a difficult time allowing our lives to be threatened repeatedly."

"Mr. Miller is a brave, principled man," Tap began. "It's certainly not the way I would handle the matter—but my background is not gentle and spiritual, rather violent and worldly. I respect his determination."

Lucinda Miller looked straight at Pepper. "It will be of some comfort to me as a widow, I am sure, to remember my husband as a faithful and principled man. However, if I could have my choice, I would choose not to be a widow."

"How can we help you, Mrs. Miller?" Pepper asked.

"I pray that God—and Mr. Miller—will forgive me for what I'm about to say. I have no right to ask this. I do not want you to jeopardize your own safety. You have a lovely wife and children to think of yourself."

"What exactly are you asking Tap to do?" Pepper inquired.

Lucinda Miller pulled her fingers apart and wrapped her arms across her chest tightly. "I am asking . . . if Mr. Andrews would—or could . . . go up to the farm and check on Ezra and Peter."

"Is that all?" Tap pressed.

"And," she gasped, "and use . . . whatever force necessary to ensure that my husband and my eldest child do not get murdered."

She dropped her face into her hands and began to weep. Pepper could see Mrs. Miller's chest heave as her sobs filled the room. Scooting over on the sofa, Pepper felt her unbuttoned dress slip slightly down off her shoulder. She tugged it back into place and wrapped her arm around the woman's shoulder and began to rock her back and forth.

"What can I do, darlin'?" Tap asked. "You know I'll go up there."

"I know." Pepper nodded. "Maybe you could go do some book work . . . or go work your leather or something."

"Think I'll step out to the barn. . . . Are you sure you'll be all right?"

"Yes." Pepper tried to wipe tears from her own eyes.

By nine o'clock the only light shining at the Slash-Bar-4 head-quarters was the kerosene lamp in the living room of the big house. Mrs. Miller and her children had turned their lamp off around 8:00. Howdy Renten had doused his about 8:30. Mr. and Mrs. Odessa had not bothered even turning one on. Only a small plume of smoke from the cottage chimney signaled they were home.

Tap and Pepper sat on the couch staring at the flames in the huge rock fireplace. His bootless feet were propped up on a three-legged stool. Wearing a flannel nightgown covered by a flannel robe, Pepper sat crosswise on the couch, her feet in Tap's lap. Through two pair of heavy socks, he rubbed her feet.

"Well, Mr. Tap Andrews, what are you going to do tomorrow?"

He rested his head on the brown leather sofa back and stared at the pounded copper ceiling. "Me and Odessa will ride up to Cedar Mesa to check some boundary markers. And as long as we're in the neighborhood, ride a few more hours to Badger Canyon."

"Will you use your gun if necessary?"

"To protect myself? Certainly."

"No . . . will you use it to protect Mr. Miller?"

"It's not that easy, is it?" He sighed. "I mean, my natural reaction is to say, 'Yes, of course,' but Mr. Miller doesn't want me to do that."

"Mrs. Miller does."

"That's why this is so difficult. If I have to shoot someone to save Mr. Miller's life, it will offend him greatly."

"So what will you do?"

"I imagine I'll lay awake half the night trying to figure that out."

"What are you going to do the other half of the night?" Pepper teased.

"Rub your back, darlin', rub your back."

"Andrews, you're a sweet-talkin' romeo. You knew exactly what I wanted to hear."

He glanced over at the sparkling green eyes. "Oh, yeah, that's me—Mr. Smooth Talker himself."

"Well, Mr. S. T., how about just picking me up and carrying me to bed?"

His brown eyes grew wide. "You want me to do what?"

"That was a joke, dear."

"Oh . . . yeah, well, if you wanted me to, I'm sure I could do it."

"Mrs. Miller isn't the only one afraid of becoming a widow. I think I'll walk."

The clouds were scattered over the winter blue sky. A mud-drying wind whipped along from the west. It was cold and biting, but it wasn't winter. Just a hint of what was to come.

Tap rode out from the house alone—his gray felt hat pulled low, a black silk bandanna double-wrapped at his neck, wool vest buttoned tight, canvas coat buttoned only at the top, leather gauntlets covering his hands. Behind the rolled binding of the deep-seated cantle was a bedroll, slicker, grub bag, and worn Winchester box that contained fifty reloaded .44-40 cartridges.

Roundhouse's breath fogged the air like smoke. The big horse wanted to prance in the crisp morning air, but Tap held him back and made him walk. "We've got a long day, Roundy—mighty long day. Don't wear yourself out."

'Course it would have gone by a little quicker if Lorenzo had come along. But I'm not going to go banging on the door and disturbing them. Howdy said they ate the supper he left on their porch, but other than that, no one's seen them since they got back to the ranch. Pepper said they needed time to settle into a new routine. But how much settlin' do two people need?

Tap rode all the way to Cedar Mesa before he stopped to build a fire and eat. The hard rain of the previous day had erased all distinguishable tracks. Following landmarks that he remembered from the previous week, Tap headed in the general direction of Badger Canyon.

The sun peeked between the clouds long enough for Tap to see that it was three-quarters across the sky. He cut across the top of a north- and south-running dry wash. It branched off from a west-running creek that he was fairly confident led to the box canyon that walled in Miller's homestead. The dry gulch offered a narrow trail leading south. Rain had washed it out except for a curved path along an overhanging basalt outcropping. Tap rode down to the overhang and studied the sign.

Two ponies wearing shoes . . . maybe yesterday . . . Ezra and Peter brought their wagon. Could be some of those trying to run them off. I ought to ride out on that trail. It must lead back to the river sooner or later.

Tap pulled his '73 rifle out of the scabbard and laid it across his lap. He kept Roundhouse at a steady walk. "Got to take it easy, big boy. Might be a welcoming committee waitin' for us."

Reaching the creek again, he turned east and stayed on the south side, even though the only trail was on the north side of the creek. Meandering through brush, trees, and tiny meadows, he picked his way up the five-foot-wide shallow creek.

"Well, Roundy, we ought to be gettin' close to where they jumped us last week. It all looks a little different in the daylight—from this side of the crick."

An hour later Tap caught a glimpse of something red up on the slope of the mountain. Without lifting the rifle from his lap, he cocked the hammer. A cartridge was already in the chamber. Roundhouse lifted his nose and turned his head from one side to the other.

"What's up there, boy? It's red, whatever it is. . . . Nice and slow now. We'll have to ride up out of this brush to get a good look."

Tap rode into the trees on the south. Coming out behind a clump of small yellow-leafed quaking aspen, he surveyed the scene below. Two men, one wearing a red bandanna, leaned against neighboring trees. Their hands and feet were strapped around the trunks.

Well, you boys got yourself in a fix. Can't tell who you are from here, but you aren't Miller and his son, I can see. Could be Indian bait—waitin' for someone to try and rescue them. That's an old

*Apache trick . . . but this is such a remote place, it would be like
fishin' for trout in a mud hole.*

*'Course they could be fakin' it. Maybe they saw me comin' and
wanted to sucker me in. They could have hid their horses behind
them cedars.*

*You're too suspicious, Andrews. Pappy Divide always said I
was the most suspicious man in the West.*

'Course Pappy's dead now.

Tap broke out of the aspens, his rifle aimed at the bright red
bandanna, still a hundred yards away.

"Hey, mister!" came a shout. "We need some help!"

"Man, are we glad to see you! You saved our lives!"

The voices sounded familiar.

Tap raised his rifle to his shoulder and continued to walk
Roundhouse toward the men. He could hear every broken twig
beneath the big horse's hooves and the tinkle of the quietly flowing creek. He could see with crystal clarity three small cedar trees
on the extreme left of his vision, a cobweb-laced bush that rustled
in the wind on the far right, and everything in between, including
the nervous eyes of the two bound men. He could feel his feet
mash against the tapadera-covered stirrups, the alert but not
alarmed tenseness of his arms, neck, and eyes. The air smelled
fresh, new. Each breath carried a taste of anticipation.

*Lord, I don't know if it's my old nature galloping away with
me or if it's a gift You've provided, but when the guns are drawn,
when the confrontation comes, it's as if everything becomes
clearer to discern.*

"Well, boys, isn't this a surprise?" he called out as he approached.
"If it isn't those famous bank robbers—Jackson and Bean."

"Andrews, don't shoot us. We're unarmed!" the one with the
bright red bandanna hollered. His coat was unbuttoned, and his
hat lay in the dirt beside him.

"Think about it, Jackson—if I shoot the two of you and pack
your carcasses back to town and give 'em the money, I'll be
declared a hero. Someone would probably buy me supper ever'
day for a year."

"But we ain't got the money! They bushwhacked us!" Jackson complained.

"They double-crossed us," Bean fussed as he tugged at the stiff three-eighths-inch, four-strand maguey rope that laced his hands to the trunk of the tree.

"Double-crossed?"

"Be quiet, Bean!"

"Quiet? We was comin' to join up with 'em. They was supposed to be our friends, and they robbed us and took our bank money. Left us here for dead. I don't owe them nothin'!" Bean's new wool suit was ripped at the knee, his wool coat flapped open, and his tie dangled around his neck.

"Quiet! They could have just been funnin' us and plan to come back later and set us free." Jackson sported a mustache and a two-day beard.

"Well, it ain't one bit fun!" the clean-shaven Bean replied.

"Who double-crossed you?"

"Don't tell him nothin'!" Jackson shouted.

"You're crazy!" Bean shouted. "There ain't goin' to be no one else come along and cut us free. So he might as well shoot us. It beats lettin' the wolves and bears gnaw on our bones or the Indians usin' us for target practice!"

"Who double-crossed you?" Tap repeated.

"It was that Yellow Sash bunch."

"They rode up here? I heard they hide out on the Crow Reserve."

"Crow Reserve, nothin'. They live up there in the old Pothook-H headquarters. They pay an Indian to hold their relay team on the reservation. Then they sneak across the river and ride up here. By day they pretend to be cowhands. At night they go stealin'. No wonder they don't want any neighbors. Mister, I'll make you a deal."

"Shut up, Bean!"

"Jackson, you can stay tied to a tree if you want. I'm makin' me a deal."

"What kind of deal?" Tap asked. He remained in the saddle,

only a few feet from the bound men. The barrel of his cocked rifle pointed down at Bean's head.

"You cut us free, and then we'll track 'em down, shoot them skunks, and get the bank money back. You can have half the money, and we'll take the other and our rigs. Then we'll light shuck for Wyomin'. If Jackson don't want to go, you can leave him tied to the tree. What do you say? A thousand bucks is a lot of money."

"Two thousand is even more. Why don't I just keep it all?"

"You goin' to take on the whole Yellow Sash bunch by yourself? You're crazier than we are!"

"You two have tried to sneak up and shoot me in the dark, and you tried to bash in my head with shovel handles. I've got a real good idea I'd have a better chance at the Yellow Sash gang with the two of you tied to this tree. But I'm not after any gang—just on a visit to see some friends."

"You ain't goin' to leave us here, are you?" Bean protested.

"I don't reckon I have any choice. I can't take you with me on one horse. I can't turn you loose because you robbed some good people who were countin' on that money. But I'll tell you what I'll do. If things go according to plan, I'll be comin' back this way— maybe with a wagon. If you're still here, I'll cut you down and haul you into town to stand trial."

"We'll be dead in two days."

"You might be surprised how tough you are. Besides, you might figure out a way to bust that old maguey. It's not the toughest rope in the world."

"We can't go without water!" Bean complained.

Tap paused.

Proud, stupid, scared, foolish—I don't know what to do with 'em, Lord. Keep 'em alive until I come this way with a wagon.

He climbed down off Roundhouse and shoved the rifle back into the scabbard. "Well, you boys caught me on a generous day."

"You going to cut us loose after all?"

"Not hardly . . . but I will give you a drink." Tap pulled his canteen off his saddle horn.

"Cut my hands loose and let me drink," Bean called out. "My wrists are killin' me."

"Afraid not. The hands stay tied."

"I cain't drink without usin' my hands."

"Sure you can, Bean. You have a low opinion of your own ability." Tap tugged the cork out of his leather-wrapped canteen. "Open up and don't take it into your lungs and drown."

When Bean lifted up his mouth, his hat tumbled to the ground. He took a mouthful of water that spilled down on his neck and shirt. Tap waited for him to swallow and then gave him another drink.

"Thanks, mister. I cain't say I'd do the same for you if the tables was turned. Could you jam my hat back on my head? I feel a little warmer with my hat on."

Tap turned to the other man. "Jackson, you want a drink or not?"

"What I want is to live long enough to kill you," he threatened.

"Mister, I'm gettin' on that horse and ridin' up the line to take care of some business. Once I hit that saddle, I'm not gettin' down to give you a drink. I don't need a threat or a curse. You want a drink or not?"

Jackson glared, then looked down at the ground. "Yeah," he mumbled. Tap gave him a couple of mouthfuls of water and then tapped the cork tight on the canteen. He strapped the canteen on the saddle horn and walked around to the off side of the horse.

"Mister," Jackson added in a low voice, "could you jam my hat on my head too?"

Tap scooped up the brown felt hat, brushed the dirt off the hatband, and jammed it down on Jackson's head. Then he mounted up and spun Roundhouse several circles to the right. Pulling up on the reins, Tap glanced back at the two men.

"Boys, I meant what I said. If you're still here when I come back through, I'll see you get taken into Billings."

"We cain't stay like this two or three days!"

"You didn't leave me any other choice. That maguey rope is goin' to be the easiest to break when it gets real cold—say about sunup. Save your strength until then. Then yank it just as hard as you can in one quick motion. I've never owned a McGee that couldn't be busted when you tied it hard and fast. If you do get free, build yourself a fire and warm up before you try hikin' out of these mountains. Too much cold will kill you quicker than the wolves or Indians."

Tap touched his engraved silver Spanish rowels to Roundhouse's flanks and trotted up the creek.

Lord, that's the second time in two days I've been in a situation where there was nothin' I could do about the matter.

Tap spotted a thin column of smoke coming from the Miller homestead the moment he entered the wide, flat box canyon. From a distance he didn't know if it was the smoldering ruins of the barn or a cook fire. Not knowing who or what to expect, Andrews kept his rifle across his lap. The eight-and-a-half-pound Winchester rested heavy on the cold, stiff duckings.

He was still three hundred yards away when he spotted animals in a makeshift corral behind the collapsed and charred remains of the barn. The house consisted of a log base four feet tall on all four sides, with a slot for a front door—nothing else.

At one hundred yards Tap reined up and hollered, "Ezra, it's me—Tap Andrews! I'm coming in!"

Peter's blond head peeked up over the wall first, followed by the full-bearded face of his father. The young boy vaulted the wall of the house and scampered out to Tap.

"Hi, Mr. Andrews! We rounded up most of the animals. Only the goats and one hog is missing!"

"That's good, son. Glad to hear that."

Ezra Miller, wearing dark trousers and a dirty white shirt under his unbuttoned heavy blanket coat, walked through the doorway of the wall and out into the dirt yard. "Is everything all right? Lucinda and the children are safe?"

"Yep. Angelita has the kids all organized and attendin' her school," Tap reported.

"Then why did you come out? I told you I had to do this myself," Miller insisted.

"Well, Ezra, I was checkin' out Cedar Mesa and sightin' in the property line when I ran across the trail of a couple riders . . . so

I naturally followed them up the mountain a ways. The next thing I knew, the surroundings started lookin' familiar, so I thought why not stop by and have supper with Ezra and Peter?"

"Brother Andrews, you are too honest a man. Windy stories like that sound off-tune. You've got a bedroll and grub sack. You didn't just stray a little off course."

"Well, Mrs. Miller was gettin' a little worried, and I offered to bring her a report. The part about the riders is true. There are two bank robbers tied up in the pine trees down the crick about four miles."

"Bank robbers?" Peter gasped.

"They robbed a bank in Billings last Saturday."

"And you caught them?" Peter Miller's eyes grew wide.

"Someone robbed them and tied them to trees."

"And you left them there?" Ezra asked.

"I couldn't put them on my pony, and I didn't know what I'd find at your place. I gave them some water and told 'em I'd come back for them and see that they get to stand trial in Billings."

"Hitch up the team, Peter. We'll go get those men," Mr. Miller instructed.

"What are we going to do with them here?" Peter asked.

"They can be fed and allowed to lay down and sleep. Where did you say they were?"

"If you've got the time, so do I," Andrews suggested. "Let's all go. How are things here?"

"Oh, we haven't had any trouble . . . since this morning."

"This morning?"

"Like Peter said, we rounded up most of the animals yesterday during the rainstorm. But this morning, a couple hours after day-break, two of the Pothook-H men rode right up to the barn and shot a yearling calf. They said they'd come back every hour and shoot an animal until we pulled out."

"They said that after the animals were all gone, if we were still here, we'd be the target," Peter added.

"What happened then?" Tap questioned.

"We watched them down in the aspen. Looked to me like another rider came in, and after a quick conversation, they all rode off. We haven't seen them since. I think perhaps they decided harassing us was a waste of time."

"What they decided was that they ought to go back down the hill and lift those bank robbers' poke."

Ezra Miller assisted Peter in hitching up the team to the farm wagon. "You think they'll be comin' back then?"

"I think they absolutely don't want any witnesses up in these mountains. They plan on gettin' you out of here one way or another."

"And I say you have much too negative a view of mankind. They are creations of God, just as you and I."

"Oh, I don't argue with that. That calf they shot was a part of God's creation too. But I believe some men have twisted and warped God's design so bad that they are almost beyond repair."

"I'm glad you said almost, Brother Andrews. God's redemptive power is beyond our imagination."

"Well, sir . . . I'm livin' proof of that. But these boys won't hesitate to shoot you if they get a chance. It's just a matter of time."

"I think you're dead wrong—"

Wood exploded from right behind where Peter sat. A rifle report followed.

"Leave the team! Get behind that barrier!" Tap shouted as Peter dove behind the half-built log wall. Andrews galloped his horse to the corral and turned him out, letting the reins loop over the saddle horn.

Another shot echoed through the canyon. Tap sprinted back to the wall of the house where Ezra Miller and his son crouched.

"I'm goin' to drive your team back to the corral so you won't lose a horse!" Tap shouted.

"Be careful!" Miller called out.

Tap popped over the wall and fired three quick shots into the aspen grove.

"Brother Andrews, please don't fire that gun at another human on my farm! I don't need a lethal weapon for my protection!"

Tap fired two more shots into the trees and ran for the wagon. "Well, I do, Brother Miller. I do!"

7

Several bullets tunneled into the hard-packed mud around the wagon as Tap Andrews slapped leathers against the two frightened draft horses. The wagon rattled back to the temporary corral, partially hidden from the gunmen in the woods by the steep-sided canyon.

Tap dove over the back wall of the house, barely avoiding the deep pit that was to become a root cellar, and crawled up to Ezra and Peter Miller. He could feel the water and mud ooze through the knees of his canvas ducking trousers. A single shot rang out from the grove of trees. Tap had no idea where the bullet hit.

"Mr. Andrews, the shooting has slowed down. Did you hit one of them?" Peter asked.

"Not likely. At this range it takes a careful shot. All I was tryin' to do was get them to hide so I could drive the team to safety. 'Course there's always the chance of a stray bullet wingin' someone. But that doesn't happen very often. Nine out of ten men couldn't hit you at this range if you stood up and waved your arms."

"Why do we need to hide like this then?"

"Might be that tenth man out there."

"What do you think we should do now?" Peter asked.

"That's up to your father. I'm just a neighbor on a visit. This is his place."

No more shots rang out from the woods, but all three continued to crouch behind the partial log wall. Tap held his rifle. The

lever was checked, the h
finger on his right han
trigger. *They're prob*
have about five min

With thick wool
hair uncombed, Pet
you do if this were

Tap leaned his b   ᴜ⸱   aɴ
didn't feel like I cou⸱. ⸱a⸱⸱ ⸱⸱⸱ ⸱⸱aight up, ⸱   until dark,
build a little bait fire until they started sneakin in to shoot, and
then I'd hide in the dark and pick them off one at a time."

"It's not right to take another man's life," Ezra Miller lectured
as he sat on the dirt floor of the living room.

"I ain't arguin' theology. I don't know next to beans when it
comes to doctrine." Tap pulled cartridges from his bullet belt and
shoved them into the breech-loading chamber. "But each man is
accountable to the Lord for his actions. For me . . . well, when
some hombre starts tryin' to take my life or the life of innocent
people, he's forfeited his right of protection from the Scriptures.
The way I reckon, he's voluntarily moved himself into the 'eye-for-
an-eye' category."

"Brother Andrews," Miller continued, "when you pick up a
firearm and aim it at another, even in defense, you're no longer
trusting God for your deliverance."

All three flinched when two bullets slammed into the eighteen-
inch logs in the front wall. The report from the rifles was simul-
taneous with the impact of the bullets.

"Aren't they getting closer?" Peter asked.

"Yep." Tap kept behind the barrier but searched for better protection. *They're spreadin' out and movin' in. Only two of 'em are*
shootin'. "Well, Ezra, what if it was God who gave me the ability
to shoot this gun? Then when I use it to protect the innocent, I
reckon I'm part of God's deliverance."

"That's absurd—perhaps even blasphemy. The Almighty
doesn't need a .44-40 to accomplish His will."

"I don't surmise He does. But sometimes He uses such things."
Two more shots slammed into the log barrier. "I just read the

other night that King Ahab was killed by a random arrow. The Lord could have struck him down on the spot, but He used that arrow instead. Some old boy had to pick up his bow and sling that arrow into the air. Could be ever' once in a while He does things that way."

"That's entirely different," Miller insisted.

"Well, sir, that's where we disagree. One thing I can tell you for sure is that these men are gettin' closer, and we better find some better shelter, because it sounds like they aim to kill us this time."

"If you hadn't shot at them, they wouldn't have felt the need to keep on shooting," Miller insisted.

Tap just stared at Ezra Miller. *Lord, idealism only succeeds in an ideal world. This isn't it. He's goin' to get himself killed, and he won't let me keep it from happenin'! There's got to be a way to keep him alive!*

"Ezra, I'm sorry you feel like I endangered you and Peter. That was not my intention." Tap stared back at the bluff and the livestock. "Here's what I can do. I'm goin' to ride straight out that creek. They'll see me, and they'll hear my rifle thunder. They'll know it's just you and Peter back here. If they refuse to shoot an unarmed man and boy, you'll survive. 'Course your animals won't get that break. You'll lose 'em all—even those big draft horses."

"If they had wanted to kill us," Miller insisted, "they would have done it before now."

"You could be right about that." Tap searched the surrounding yard and then pointed at the big hole at the other end of the house. "You two stay down in the root cellar up against the west wall. When you hear shootin' from the trees, climb in that wagon and drive all night to get back to that family of yours. This is a big country out here. Find yourself another piece of it."

Miller held his hat in his hand and pointed his wide, stubby finger at Tap. "I'm not leavin'. I think I made that clear to you already."

"I'm not the one you have to convince," Tap explained. "I think these boys are hidin' after robbin' and rustlin'. They figure if they run you out, you'll let others know this isn't a place for nesters. But if they up and kill you . . . well, the U.S. Marshal might ride up here and discover their hideout."

Ezra Miller slumped back against the wall. "In that case we don't have to worry about being killed."

"When I dive over the back, jump in the cellar. Miller, your logic works only as long as you want to be burnt out, shot at, and have your animals killed. And then when a couple of these boys get really drunk, they'll forget their plan and shoot you two down anyway."

"I think it's time you left." Miller's wide neck turned scarlet. "You're needlessly frightening the lad."

Tap turned to the boy. "Peter, your daddy's a brave man. Don't you ever think otherwise. And I'm surely sorry to cause you worry. But the only assistance I can offer you is from the barrel of a gun and a lifetime of livin' in the West. If there comes a time you need my help, let me know."

"Brother Andrews, I don't wish to sound ungrateful for your offer of help." Ezra Miller stared back up the canyon to the north behind the cabin. "I know it's sincere, but it's misguided. It's just something I can't be a part of."

"May the Lord be gracious to you. I'll tell Mrs. Miller you are well."

"Are you really going to ride straight at those trees?" Peter called out.

"Yep."

"You'll be right out in the open! I never heard of anyone doing something like that!"

"Neither have they, Peter. Neither have they."

Tap dove over the back wall and rolled in the hoof-packed mud as two shots rang out. One came from the north, the other from the south. *This will work if they've flanked the crick bed and there are only a couple of 'em. 'Course if they were smart, they'd have left one hiding in those trees. Boys, I'm countin' on you not being that smart.*

Tap reached Roundhouse without any more shots being fired. The corral was protected from the sight of the gunmen by a granite cliff that jutted out toward the house. The big gray horse spun to the right as Tap cinched down the Visalia saddle and tried to jam his right foot in the off-side tapadera-covered stirrup.

"This is no time for games, horse! You're goin' to have to run like the wind!" Tap pulled himself into the saddle, shoved his rifle in the scabbard, and continued to circle the horse to the right. He pulled his Colt .44 from his holster and gripped it with his right hand. He circled the horse behind the burned barn and galloped him straight toward the back of the house.

"Come on, Roundy, now's the time to show your stuff!"

The big gelding leaped the back wall of the house, trampled across the dirt floor that was once the living room, and jumped the front wall. Ezra and Peter Miller huddled down in the eight-foot-deep hole that took up half the cabin.

He saw a puff of gunpowder from the short pine trees on the right and heard the report of the gun, but he couldn't tell how close the bullet came. His two-inch Spanish rowels raked the big horse. They rumbled up the north side of the creekbed like a locomotive an hour behind schedule. Several more shots rang out. Water splashed in the creek ten feet behind him.

He refrained from returning fire and bore down on the clump of aspens at the jog in the creek. Four horses were tied behind the trees. They danced and pawed and tugged at their lead ropes when they heard the galloping hooves.

Are there four of 'em?

Two shots rang out from down the creek and splintered the white trunks of the aspens thirty yards behind Tap.

If I take their horses, they'll turn on Ezra and Peter and go after the wagon. If I leave their horses, they'll come after me.

Shots continued to come closer.

"Well, Roundy, only two of 'em are shootin' at us. Those two horses with loose cinches probably haven't been ridden in a while. I surmise they belong to Jackson and Bean."

Tap jumped down, untied all four horses, and slapped two in the rump until they trotted off toward the trees. He fired two shots in the general direction of the southern gunman and two toward the north. Then he remounted and led the other two horses behind him as he cantered down the creekbed. Well hidden in the brush, he stopped and pulled his Winchester. Flipping up the long-range peep sight on the upper tang, he sighted in the two saddle horses that now grazed only a few yards from the aspen.

A man in a long wool coat broke out of the woods and ran toward the horses. Tap squeezed the trigger and sent rocks flying between the man and the horses. The animals panicked and sprinted into the trees. The man dove to the dirt and fired a couple of wide shots in Tap's direction.

"That ought to keep them all thinkin' for a few minutes anyway. Come on, Roundy, we've got a couple of outlaws to round up."

If I know those Sash boys, they'll be as mad as a broke cowboy in a dance hall. They'll catch those horses and come after me. It'll be dark in an hour, so I'll just have to see how good they can track.

Tap led the horses straight up the creekbed for a couple of miles. Even in the shadows of an October night, he spotted the red bandanna still flagged around Jackson's neck. Tap pulled his Colt and cocked the hammer as he approached.

"You got our horses!" Bean yelled. "I didn't figure we'd ever see you again!"

Tap rode up next to the bound bank robbers and then turned around to see if he was being followed. "This is your lucky day."

"Did you kill 'em?" Bean quizzed.

"Nope."

Jackson's eyes narrowed. "Did you get the money?"

"I figure that's back at the Pothook-H headquarters by now. I told you I was goin' to see a friend. It just happens I came upon these ponies. For the life of me, I can't figure why they were keepin' your horses out here."

"Maybe they were coming back for us, like I said," Jackson suggested.

"And maybe they wanted to ride you down to the river and shoot you. They surely didn't want the U.S. Marshal comin' up here lookin' for you."

"Cut us down, Andrews. I've got no feelin' left in my hands or my feet," Bean protested.

"Boys, we're ridin' on in to the ranch tonight. A couple of the gang will be comin' after us. There's no time for a fire. Does that trail you came up lead back to the Yellowstone?"

"Yeah." Bean nodded as Tap cut the skinny rope that held him. Andrews kept his gun on the man, who stumbled and collapsed to the ground. He shoved the gun into the back of Bean's neck.

"Now listen, if you try to escape, I'll shoot you dead. You'd be a lot easier to pack out of here strapped to your saddle. But if you mind your manners, I'll let you ride out. It's up to you—make it easy on me, or make it easy on you. Which is it going to be?"

"I can't even move my hands," Bean groaned. "I won't cause you no trouble."

"Which horse is yours?"

"The bay."

"Put your hands behind your back," Tap ordered.

"My hands is numb."

"Good, then this won't hurt."

Within minutes Bean was mounted on his horse, hands tied behind his back. Tap then took a rope off the bank robber's saddle and tied it to the saddle horn. Leaving a four-foot section, he tied the other end around Bean's neck with a slip knot.

"You cain't do that. If I fall off, I'll hang myself."

"Yeah, I reckon you're right," Tap agreed. "And if you try to jump off, the same thing will happen."

"You ain't goin' to do that to me!" Jackson called out.

Tap whipped around with his Colt and jammed the barrel against Jackson's neck. "Why don't you make a run for it and save me a lot of hassle?"

"I'm tied to a tree!"

"I can take care of that!" Tap shoved his revolver back into the holster, pulled his knife out of his boot, and sliced the ropes that held Jackson. The man staggered at Tap and threw a wild punch. Stepping back, Tap met the lunging man with an uppercut to the chin.

Stunned, Jackson stood straight up for a second, but he collapsed on his back when Tap's roundhouse right slammed into the left side of his jaw.

Tap rolled Jackson over and tied his hands and feet together. Then he hefted the robber like a sack of wheat and flopped him across the saddle on his stomach. Taking some of the sliced-up maguey, Tap had lashed Jackson in place by the time the man came around.

"I can't ride this way, Andrews!" Jackson growled as he tried to kick his feet free.

"Why, sure you can. You boys just lack self-confidence. The only thing you have to worry about is fallin' off. So try and stay in the center of that saddle."

Tap tied the reins of Bean's horse to the cantle strings of Jackson's saddle. He did the same between Roundhouse and Jackson's horse and then led the parade up the side of the mountain under an increasingly starlit October night.

"Let me loose, Andrews!" Jackson yelled.

"Now you two ought to be thankful. You're not still tied to a tree, I didn't coldcock you, and you aren't dead. You got to admit, that's better than you figured."

"We'll kill you, Andrews! We'll get away, and we'll kill you!" Jackson threatened.

"Boys, the other day I spotted Indian pony tracks on this trail. I think it's a hunting route for them. If you keep yellin', you're liable to draw attention. And I'm tellin' you right now, if they show up, I'll drop the two of you and ride right on out of here. It could be to your advantage to keep quiet."

They did.

Tap didn't know if Jackson and Bean got any sleep during the night, but he did. Several times along the trail he caught himself waking up from a short nap, only to find Roundhouse continuing his long-legged plod.

Twice they stopped and huddled around a campfire, once at the edge of Cedar Mesa and again along the Yellowstone. Jackson settled down and rode most of the way sitting in the saddle like Bean. Both had ropes tied hard and fast to the saddle horn and looped around their necks.

A cloud cover blew in after midnight, and the trail became harder to follow. Tap circled the ranch and entered the headquarters from the river, hoping to lose the pursuers along the way. He was counting on them wanting to visit Starke and Cantrell's or just giving up and returning to the Pothook-H. In the darkness Tap had no way of determining if they were being followed.

The first gray light of morning found them walking their exhausted horses up the drive to Slash-Bar-4 headquarters. Even in the dim light, Tap could see the familiar silhouettes of the big house and barn . . . and tepee.

A tepee? What's that doing here?

"You got Indians livin' here, Andrews?" Bean questioned.

"Eh . . . they're just visitin'," he mumbled.

This doesn't look like a ranch. It looks like a traders' fort! I was only gone one day.

A thin gray column of smoke rose from the cook shack. Tap could see lantern light in the west window. His rifle in his right hand, he circled around by the unpainted wood-framed building.

"Howdy, I need a little help out here!" he hollered.

Clothed in a Hudson Bay blanket coat and moccasins to his knees, Howdy Renten stepped out on the porch. He stared at the two bound men.

"You want me to feed 'em or hang 'em?" he asked.

"Neither. Help me put those iron hobbles on—"

"You ain't puttin' no hobbles on me!" Jackson shouted.

"In that case," Tap said shrugging, "hang 'em."

"Wait!" Bean hollered. "You didn't hear me complain none!"

"I'm goin' to kill you, Andrews!" Jackson growled.

Tap looked over at Renten. "I've kept these two bank robbers alive all night, and all they do is complain."

Howdy Renten stepped to the edge of the porch and squinted. "These the ones that took potshots at us, knifed your arm, and robbed the Billings bank?"

"Yeah, but they went up in the mountains and got themselves robbed."

"Robbers gettin' robbed?" Howdy mumbled as he marched the two men over to the blacksmith's shop. "A man can't rob a bank and ride away anymore. Someone else comes along and takes your hard-earned money. What's this land comin' to?"

Tap held the rifle on them while Howdy fastened the heavy iron hobbles and chains on both their right ankles.

"Why did you do it that way?" Bean complained. "Now one of us has to walk backwards wherever we go."

"You catch on fast." Tap slipped the ropes off their necks but left their hands tied. "You boys head for the barn, and I'll chain you up in a stall with clean straw. Howdy will give you a pan of grub, and in a bit one of us will drive you into Billings. Boys, you're goin' to get out of the cold, get some rest, and be fed. That's a lot more than you deserve."

"I'm still goin' to kill you," Jackson growled.

Tap pulled the saddles and curried the horses as Renten finished chaining Jackson and Bean to an empty stall.

"Well," Howdy drawled, "ain't you goin' to ask me about that lodge out there?"

"Oh, I figured you'd tell me when you were ready." Tap rubbed down Roundhouse with a rolled-up burlap sack.

"Don't that beat all?" Howdy said to the two chained men. "He's got a family of Crows camped out on the front porch, and he ain't even curious."

Tap let his gray felt hat drop to his back and hang by the stampede string. He rubbed the back of his neck and could feel his brown hair jammed against his coat collar. "Are they hungry?"

Howdy Renten circled Bean's horse, lifting each hoof as he went. "No, they're mad as a house cat in a stock tank."

Tap rubbed some liniment into the gelding's right foreleg. "Did we do somethin' wrong?"

"Not yet. They want you to help 'em catch somebody. He speaks mighty good English, but he don't talk much. At least, not to me."

"Why us? Why not go to the Indian Agency or the U.S. Marshal or the county sheriff?"

Renten led Bean's horse to a stall. "Well, that's what I couldn't make out. He said he'd just camp out there and wait until Tapadera Andrews got home."

"He knew my name?"

"Yep. Ain't that something? Must make you feel important."

Tap put a scoop of oats in a feed bag and fastened it on

Roundhouse's head. "Makes me feel suspicious. What else is goin' on around here?"

"Well, I hear your missus wasn't feelin' too swift yesterday. Angelita is lookin' after her. . . . Them Miller kids swarm over the whole ranch . . . and I ain't seen toe to ear of Mr. or Mrs. Odessa."

"Are you sure they came back in that carriage?" Tap stalled his big gray and ignored the glares of Jackson and Bean.

"Someone's in there talkin' and laughin' and eatin' the supper I put on the porch."

"Well, I better get up to the house and see how Mama is."

"What do you want me to do if these two try to escape?" Howdy asked.

"Shoot 'em."

Angelita was building up a fire in the rock fireplace. She jumped at the sound of the creaking front door.

"You scared me!" she choked.

"Well, it didn't seem right for a man to have to knock on his own front door. How's Mama?" Tap inquired.

"Did you see Peter Miller?"

"I heard she was a little under the weather."

"They didn't get themselves shot, did they?"

"Is she awake yet?" Tap asked. "Maybe I better go up and check on her."

"Mrs. Miller is worried sick. She just sits in the bunkhouse rocking the baby and staring out the window."

"Maybe I should take Pepper to Billings to a doctor when I take those bank robbers back."

"Did you know that a lodge of Crow Indians set up camp in the pasture yesterday?" Angelita pressed.

"I should move you both into a hotel until after that baby is born."

"They won't talk to anyone but you," she continued. "Are they friends of yours?"

Tap glanced at the stairs. "I'm going up to see Pepper. How about you boilin' some coffee for me?"

"Why don't you go up and see Mama?" Angelita offered. "I'll get some coffee boilin'."

Tap stared at Angelita's big dark eyes. They both grinned.

"I did hear what you were sayin'," Tap insisted.

She tilted her head sideways and rubbed her wide brown nose with the palm of her hand. "I know it. It's like a game. Now go on before our conversation starts making sense."

Tap poked his head into the bedroom. Pepper was in bed somewhere under a pile of quilts. She had a white lace afghan pulled over her head.

Tap stared at the room. High ceiling. White lace curtains. Polished wood floor. Braided throw rug. Wardrobe closet. Large, gold-framed picture of Yosemite Valley on the wall. Dresser with combs and brushes carefully laid out. Night stands with lanterns on both sides of the bed. A leather-seated side chair by his side. A velvet-covered bench by her side, with robe and slippers neatly in place. In the southwest corner of the room a bassinet and small wardrobe. The big oak bedposts rose up like massive tree trunks.

When Stack said he'd provide the furnishin's, he didn't cut any corners. She got exactly what she wanted. Everything in its place . . . except . . .

Tap stared at the floor-length swivel mirror that was now pointed at the wall, with nothing but varnished walnut facing the room. *Oh, one of those "no-mirror" days.*

Pepper's voice filtered out from under the covers. "Well, are you going to come in or just stand there gaping?"

"I was admirin' the view." Tap stepped lightly over toward the bed. "Ever'thin's so perfect. Only one thing missin'."

"What's that?" she asked, still staying hidden under the comforter.

"Where's that pretty yellow-haired Mrs. Andrews?"

"She went away."

"When?"

"Almost nine months ago."

"Is she comin' back?"

"I don't know. I really don't know."

"Well, if you see her, could you tell her I'm still crazy about her."

"Really?"

"Yep."

"You wouldn't like her now."

"Why's that?"

"I hear she's fat and ugly."

"She's still the purdiest thing I ever laid eyes on. And I hope she comes home soon."

"Keep talkin', cowboy. I think I hear her rig pullin' up."

"Well, now I was thinkin' last night about how I'm so happy it's scary."

Pepper refused to come out from under the covers. "Scary?"

"Yep. About a year ago I didn't worry about nothin'. I didn't have nothin'. No ranch. No beautiful wife. No baby on the way. Now I'm gettin' it all, and I have to worry about losin' it. So last night I started figurin' just how much of this I could really live without if bad times came."

"What did you decide?"

"Just you, darlin'. I couldn't survive a day without you."

"Really?"

"Yep."

"I think that blonde-haired beauty just came back home."

"Good. Is she plannin' on gettin' up?"

"No."

"Well, are you goin' to pull down those covers so I can see those sparklin' green eyes?"

"No."

"How do I know it's my Pepper-girl in there? Maybe some old gal snuck in here and is pullin' a trick on me."

"Trust me."

Tap walked around to his side of the bed and sat down on the leather-seated chair and tugged at his boots. "I've been thinkin' about takin' you and Angelita into Billings and have you stay at the London House until the baby's born. That way there will be a doctor handy in case you need some help."

"I'm not leavin' this bed until the baby's born."

"You're funnin' me . . . right?"

Pepper sighed. "Sort of. But I want the baby born on the ranch, Tap. I'm serious about that."

"I warned you, I don't know how much help I'll be to you. I've delivered calves, foals, and pigs, but I don't reckon it's the same."

"Mrs. Miller has delivered babies and midwifed for years. She said she would stay until the baby's born."

The muscles in the back of Tap's neck began to relax. "She did? Honey, that's wonderful!"

"How's Mr. Miller and young Peter?"

"Do you feel like comin' down to breakfast? I'll fill you in on ever'thing while we eat."

"Yes. I'll get myself ready."

Tap padded over to the wardrobe in his stocking feet and pulled out a shirt that was folded and stacked on the top shelf. It was identical to the one he wore. Only clean. "Did you know we've got a lodge of Crow Indians in the south pasture?"

"Yes. They came in last night and asked for you by name."

"Kind of strange, isn't it? Did you know we've got a couple of bank robbers chained to a post in the barn?"

Pepper lowered the knitted white afghan so that her green eyes peeked out. "Really?"

"Yeah. I'll have to get them to Billings." He stepped next to the bed. "Darlin', have you had your mornin' kiss?"

"You kiss fat girls?"

"Not if they have an afghan over their mouth."

Pepper slipped the afghan down to her neck. "That's it, cowboy. Everything else stays covered up."

He leaned over and pressed his still cold, chapped lips against her soft, warm ones. Then he stood up.

Pepper felt the tenseness in her neck and back start to relax. *Lord, thanks for Tap. I can never figure out how he could love me.*

"After I pull on some clean duckin's, I think I'll go talk to the Indians. You will be down for breakfast, right?"

"Yes," Pepper replied, "but you have to promise you won't look at me."

"Darlin', since the day you first rode up in Bob McCurley's carriage, I haven't been able to take my eyes off you. There's no way I could start today."

"Ooouu-whee, you're one sweet-talking cowboy. Now go on! I'm surely not going to get up with you standing there gawking."

He reached over and laid his rough, callused hand against her soft face. "You doin' okay, darlin'?"

She nodded. "Just tired, Tap . . . very, very tired."

The cold wind drifted from the west. Tap turned up the collar of his canvas coat as he hiked across the yard toward the south pasture. He stopped for a moment in front of the cottage and thought briefly about rapping on the door.

"Mr. Andrews?"

It was a quiet, yet firm voice that called from the porch of the bunkhouse across the barren dirt yard. He abandoned any idea of checking on Lorenzo and Selena. "Good mornin', Mrs. Miller." He tipped his hat toward the short woman with brown hair pulled back behind her head.

"How is Mr. Miller and my Peter?"

"Doin' fine, Mrs. Miller. They caught most of the animals and are working on rebuilding the house and barn."

"Have they had any trouble?"

"Eh . . . well, not too much."

"Did he get angry about you comin' to help?"

"I reckon he didn't appreciate it. Said I was interfering."

"What kind of trouble did they have?" she asked.

"That bunch at the Pothook-H shot your calf. That's about all . . . so far. I offered to stick around, but he wouldn't hear of it. Said my guns attract too much gunfire. He could be right about that."

Lucinda Miller wrapped her arms around her chest and held herself tight. "We probably should be there with them."

"I'll be happy to take you back over if that's what you want, but you're welcome to stay here as long as you need to."

"Oh, I can't leave. I promised to help Mrs. Andrews deliver that baby of yours."

"I'm surely grateful for that, ma'am. We could use the help. But you have to do what's best for your family. We can make it if you need to go."

"Mr. Andrews, having your wife need me and the thought of bringing a new life into the world gives me an excuse to keep my other children out of danger. Don't you see?" Narrow, frightened dark eyes searched for Tap's approval. "Yes, for your wife's sake, I need to stay here!"

"I believe you're right, ma'am. I'm sure Ezra will send for you all when it's safe. Until then we surely do need you here."

"Well." She rolled her eyes as if thinking it over and then nodded. "That's what neighbors are for, Mr. Andrews. I'll certainly stay here until that baby is born."

"I appreciate it, Mrs. Miller." Tap tipped his hat. "Ma'am, I've got a couple bank robbers chained up in the barn. Tell the children I don't want any of them goin' in there unless me, Howdy, or Lorenzo are with them."

"Certainly." Mrs. Miller nodded. "By the way, how are Mr. and Mrs. Odessa? Angelita's told us about them, but we haven't met."

"Now I can't rightly say, ma'am. I haven't seen 'em since they got home. But neither of them have commenced to complain, so I surmise ever'thin's just fine."

"And what about those Indians? Should I keep the children away from them too?"

"I don't think that's a problem, but I'm headin' out to check on them. I expect they'll move on today. Is ever'thin' all right in the bunkhouse?"

"It's very sufficient. Your Angelita converted one end of it to a schoolhouse. She has all the children counting to ten in Spanish now."

"She's probably the only eleven-year-old schoolteacher in the territory."

"Or the nation."

"Good day, Mrs. Miller."

"Good day, Mr. Andrews. Thank you for looking in on my Ezra and Peter."

The tall, bleached deerhide covered tepee was pitched about twenty feet on the south side of the split-rail fence that surrounded the whole headquarters area. The opening faced the east. Two buckskins and a paint pony were tethered west of the tepee. A small fire blazed out in front of the flap. A buffalo-robed woman scurried back inside as Tap approached.

He had just climbed the fence when a man stepped out of the tepee and stalked toward him. The Indian was tall and thin but strong-shouldered. His coal-black hair was cut straight and hung to his collar, and his bangs almost reached his eyes. A beaded leather band was wrapped around his head. He wore tan canvas duckings like Tap and a long blue U.S. Cavalry coat over his deerskin shirt. His moccasins were laced up to his knees. He had a knife strapped to his braided horsehair belt, but no firearm was visible. He was somewhere between twenty-five and fifty, but Tap couldn't guess any closer than that.

"Are you Tapadera Andrews?" he asked in a deep voice.

"Yep." Tap reached out his right hand. The Indian grasped his arm halfway up to the elbow, and Tap returned the greeting.

"I'm Jesse Savage."

"Savage?"

"I like the name. For fifteen years I was called a savage. Then I went to Indian school down in Texas. I found out savage meant wild, fierce, and free. So I take it as a compliment. Would you like a cup of coffee?"

Tap glanced at a blue enameled tin pot near the fire.

"It's Arbuckles," Savage continued. "The Agency coffee isn't worth drinking."

Andrews and Savage squatted down next to the fire and sipped steaming coffee.

"What can I do for you?"

"We've got a problem over on the Reserve. A group of white outlaws have been giving us a bad name."

"This Yellow Sash gang?"

"Yeah."

"I heard they use the reservation for a horse relay and hide up in the Bull Mountains."

Savage raised his eyebrows. "So you know about that?"

"I just found out yesterday."

"Here's what's happening. Everyone thinks that they are staying on the Reserve. So we have posses, lawmen, bounty hunters, and would-be gang members combing the hills looking for them. Their horses eat on our grazing land. They shoot our antelope and what's left of the buffalo and stir up trouble among the people."

"Won't the Agency do anything about it?"

"I think the agent wants the trouble to continue so they can take this land away from us too. I hear talk of moving us to Wind River. Peace is not always as financially profitable as trouble."

"How about the U.S. Marshal's office?"

"They claim we are in partnership with the outlaws and are hiding them. They just laughed when I told them to look in the Bull Mountains."

Tap leaned a little closer to the fire. "Why did you come to me?"

"When I went to Indian school to learn to read, write, and grow tasteless white-people food like potatoes and beans, I made friends with a wild, fierce, and free half-breed Comanche warrior."

"Eagleman? Wade Eagleman?"

"His name was Two Coyotes at the time. Anyway, after several years at the school, we got jobs as scouts for General Crook. Then Two Coyotes went back to Texas to read law with some judge in San Angelo, and I came home to the Yellowstone. When I couldn't get anyone to help us, I wrote to Eagleman and asked if we could sue the government or something to keep the outlaws off our land."

"What did Wade tell you?"

"Three days ago I got a letter from him saying that the best way to handle it was to capture the Yellow Sash Gang and turn them over to the authorities. But since they were hiding off the reservation, I should recruit the best gunman in the territory, some man by the name of Tapadera Andrews who just took over the Slash-Bar-4."

Tap took a stick and idly stirred the fire. "Do you know how many are in the gang?"

"I know there are around twelve, because that's the number of relay horses they keep on our land. They are led by one named Sugar Dayton."

"Sugar Dayton! He was at my house last week claimin' to be a rancher."

"I'm sure he has cattle." The Crow warrior nodded. "Just who the cattle belong to is another question."

"Why not chase the horses off?"

"I just discovered their location last week. I want to capture the gang, not their horses."

"Well," Tap continued, "why not get a hundred of your best men, surround them when they ride in to change horses, and capture them there?"

"Because there would be shooting and killing, and the government would see it as an Indian raid on whites, and my people would be sent to live in the swamps of Florida."

"So you want to go into the mountains, capture the whole gang alive, turn them over to the U. S. Marshal's office, and have it all done with."

Savage flashed a straight-toothed smile. "Yes, that's what I want. Will you help?"

"I might. I've got some good reasons for not wantin' that gang up there too. How many men can you bring with you?"

"One."

"One?" Tap choked. "The great Crow Nation can only send two men?"

"If we are caught pursuing whites off the reservation, we will be hung. You know that. There are not many who want to run that risk. They say let the whites shoot each other."

"They have a point."

"They have never seen the swamps of Florida. I have." Jesse Savage shuddered.

Tap poured himself another cup of coffee. "So it would be just you and another man?"

"My brother. How many can you bring? Surely a big ranch like this has many men."

"Actually we aren't hirin' on many until next spring."

"At least you have two men chained in the barn, an old man who cooks like a woman, and another who lives in the small house with no lights. That makes five and two—seven. Add to them the bearded man and boy up in the cabin in Badger Canyon, and we could have nine. We could capture Yellow Sash with nine men."

"Whoa. If I can pry Lorenzo out of that cabin with no lights, we'll have two and two. Four men—that's all."

"What about the others?"

"The old man stays here to look after the place, and the two in the barn are outlaws themselves. They need to go to jail in Billings. And the man and boy in what you call Badger Canyon, well, they don't believe in usin' guns."

"We will only have four? That will make it more difficult."

"Whoa, partner, I didn't sign on yet. I'm just thinkin' about it. I'm not sure I can leave home for a while. My wife is about to have a baby."

Jesse Savage's eyes lit up. "That is good news. So is my wife. Mona, come here," he called.

The short, dark-skinned woman with beaded deerskin dress and moccasins stepped out to meet them. She had a gray army blanket draped around her shoulders. The way the dress hung, she did not look pregnant.

"Tapadera Andrews's wife is about to have a baby also."

The woman beamed but said nothing.

"Actually my Pepper is due any day now."

"So is Mona."

The woman's voice was very soft, almost musical. "I think it will be two more weeks."

"Two weeks?" Tap gasped and looked at the petite woman.

"Perhaps I could visit with your wife?" Mona Savage offered.

"I don't think that would be a good idea right now," Tap cautioned.

"She does not like to talk to Indian women?"

"No, she enjoys visitin' with Indian women. She doesn't like talking to thin women, especially thin women about to deliver a child."

8

Tap Andrews needed only six hours of sleep per night to feel rested. He couldn't remember the last time he had had six hours of sleep. He stretched out on the leather sofa in the front room right after breakfast. He had no idea how long he had been asleep, but the second he finally opened his eyes, Chester Leroy Miller leaned over the couch with his round face only inches above Tap's.

"Angelita, he's awake!" Chet screamed.

Tap leaped to his feet, searched for where he had laid his holster, and then rubbed his eyes and sighed.

"You were asleep," Chet noted in a weak, high voice.

Tap nodded, scratched his head, and tried to peer out the front window to get some bearing on the time of day. A thick cloud cover made the sun's position uncertain. The front door flew open with a bang, and Ellen Mae, Margaret Louise, and Ruth Raylene Miller marched into the room, followed by Angelita and a small Indian girl dressed in a buckskin dress.

"Good. You're finally awake," Angelita announced. "Now the play can begin in ten minutes. You'll want to help Mama out to the barn."

"What are you talkin' about? And who's that?" He pointed to the Indian girl.

"Her name's Beautiful."

"What is it?"

"I told you. That's her name. Beautiful Savage."

148   Stephen Bly

"Oh." Tap stepped to the door and pulled his hat off a peg.
"What's this about a play?"

"I wrote a play. I call it 'The Settling of the West.'"

"When did you write a play?" Tap asked.

Angelita wrinkled her nose. "This morning."

"Mornin'? What time is it?"

"It's after 3:00," she reported. All the others stood and stared
at Tap as he buckled on his holster.

"In the afternoon?" he gasped.

"Of course!" she replied in obvious disgust. "Most everyone is
already at the play. We're waiting for you to wake up. Mama said
we had to let you sleep."

"Where is Pepper?"

"Upstairs, I think."

"Did you say you're having the play in the barn? You can't do
that. I've got two bank robbers in there," Tap protested as he
jammed his hat on his head.

"Of course we'll have it in the barn. It's a morality play that I
wrote just for them. Howdy helped us fix the barn up. Mrs. Miller
and baby Matthew are already waiting. Mr. and Mrs. Savage are
coming. Now we just need you and Mama."

"You didn't invite the Odessas, did you?"

"Yes, I did. But they said they had a previous commitment and
would have to wait for the next performance. I'm thinking about
a two-week run."

Tap tried to push his eyelids up off his eyes with his fingers.
"You actually saw Selena and Lorenzo?"

"Eh, no, I didn't see them. But I talked to Miss Selena through
the door."

Tap patted Angelita's head. "Well, it's good to know they're still
livin'."

"At least one of them is." Angelita grimaced. "For all I know,
Mr. Odessa is dead. For the life of me, I can't figure out what's so
outstanding about being newlyweds."

"It's a good thing, young lady."

"We'll be waiting for you in the barn," Angelita proclaimed
and led the parade of children out of the house.

Within five minutes, Tap and Pepper were strolling across the yard toward the barn. She was wearing her brown dress. The white afghan draped her shoulders. Her left hand clutched his right arm.

"How can she write a play and get them acting it out all in the same morning?" Tap asked.

"She has an extremely busy mind." Pepper stopped Tap and caught her breath, then continued, "I'm glad the Millers are here. She'd be wearing me out if it weren't for all the children."

"She even has the little Indian girl in the play," Tap added.

"Yes . . . well, that's the only reason I agreed to hike out to the barn. Angelita says Mrs. Savage is quite far along too. At least I won't be the only expectant woman there. Maybe I won't feel so fat."

Tap shook his head and sighed.

"What's the matter?"

"Oh . . . it's—Mrs. Savage doesn't—I mean—" Tap cleared his throat. "I was a little worried about the children being out there with Jackson and Bean—the bank robbers."

"They're securely restrained, aren't they?" Pepper queried.

"Sure . . . but they might start yellin' and hollerin'."

"Angelita said she promised them that if they behaved themselves, she would give them some of the cookies she and Mr. Renten made."

"Cookies! She's goin' to give 'em cookies?"

"Come on, Mr. Andrews." Pepper pulled his arm toward the barn door. "The way I figure, Lil' Tap will be a cinch to raise after having Angelita around."

The center of the barn was the stage. The black carriage was part of the plot, as were Queenie and Albert, who were pulling back on their cotton rope headstalls and trying to locate a quick exit.

Jackson and Bean looked on from the second stall. Crates and broken chairs formed the seating where Mrs. Miller sat with little Matthew Mark in her lap. Howdy Renten, clean-shaven, sat next to her. Then Mr. and Mrs. Savage and toddler sat in the dirt near their feet. On the other side of them was a long, empty bench that had been dragged out from the bunkhouse. A cowhide pil-low was on the bench.

A young voice sailed down from the loft. "You two sit on the bench. The pillow is for Mama."

Tap stopped next to the Crow couple and introduced them to Pepper.

"Pleased to meet you, I'm sure," Pepper huffed curtly.

Both nodded their heads at Pepper but remained seated.

"And now we present," Angelita hollered from the loft, "'The Settling of the West,' written and directed by Angelita Gomez."

Pepper scrunched down on the pillow, then leaned over to Tap, and whispered, "That woman is *not* expecting!"

"She's due in two weeks or less," Tap whispered back.

"She's lying!"

Tears began to trickle down from Pepper's eyes.

"The Settling of the West" turned out to be a comedy, with most of the best lines going to the "cute, charming, and yet mys-terious" Mexican maiden Carmelita Cantina, played by the "noted actress" Angelita Gomez.

Several times Tap heard Jackson and Bean hoot and laugh. When the children finished, there was enthusiastic applause. And everyone enjoyed freshly baked cookies. Even the captive audi-ence in the horse stall.

Pepper excused herself quickly and returned to the big house. Mrs. Miller took the baby and headed back to the bunkhouse. And Mrs. Savage and her toddler retired to the tepee. That left Tap, Howdy Renten, and Jesse Savage standing at the barn door, waiting for the children to gather all their belongings.

"Are we going after Dayton and that Yellow Sash gang?" Savage asked.

"I'm still debatin'," Tap replied. He closed the big barn door as the children filed out.

"Andrews, we get our supper, don't we?" Bean hollered from the barn. "Them cookies weren't our supper, were they?"

"Two hours until suppertime!" Renten yelled.

The men walked out to the corral and stopped by the gate. Tap leaned his back against the top rail of split cedar. "It wouldn't hurt to ride up to the Pothook-H and see what we're facin'. After we count guns, we can decide if we ought to make a play. I just don't want to be gone when that baby comes."

"Yes, your wife is very fat." Jesse Savage grinned.

"Yeah, well, don't let her hear that, or you'll never live to see your children grow up," Tap cautioned.

"No," Savage replied, "there is no dishonor intended. She is ripe. She will birth the child soon."

"How do you know that?"

"My Mona said she could tell. She said not to worry. It will be at least three more days."

"Three days?" Tap groaned. "Is your Mona ever wrong?"

"No. But she's never been around white women much. My brother will be here tonight. We can leave in the morning."

"As long as we're back in two days. Does your brother know how to find you?"

"Yes, he's been here before." Jesse Savage stood on the bottom rail and stared into the corral. "Would you like to trade for those two foals?"

Tap glanced at Albert and Queenie. "Nope. When was your brother at the ranch?"

"He came with a message from me many days ago, but he found no one here."

"He looked all over?" Tap inquired.

"I suppose so."

"He didn't happen to leave all the doors and gates open, did he?"

Jesse Savage grinned from ear to ear. "He believes it will bring bad luck if he closes a gate or a door."

Tap kicked the ground near him with the toe of his boot. "Well, tell him that next time he leaves a gate or door open around here, I'll fill him with buckshot."

"I will tell him. Are we leaving in the morning then?"

"That depends on my wife's health and whether I can enlist Lorenzo Odessa."

After Savage departed, Tap accompanied Howdy to the cook-house. "You think this is just a ploy to get you away from the ranch so those Crows can form a little raiding party?" Renten asked.

Tap shot a look at the tepee. "Nope. A man doesn't put his wife and children in the line of fire, no matter what color his skin is."

"You sayin' you trust them Crows?" Renten questioned.

"I'm sayin' that whether the tribe is Mexican, Indian, white, or black, they got some that are trustworthy and some that are renegades, some that are smart and some that are dumb, some that deserve a medal and some that deserve a hangin'. I've spent my life judgin' each man one at a time. It's a pretty good system. Savage is a friend of Wade Eagleman, and Eagleman will put his life on the line for you. Did you ever notice, Howdy, how honorable men always seem to make friends with honorable men?"

"You mean like you and Odessa?"

"Yeah . . . and an old salty camp cook by the name of Howdy Renten."

"I reckon you got me on that one."

"Anyway, I won't be doin' anything before mornin'. I'll talk it over with Pepper, and we'll figure out somethin'."

No lantern light.

No starlit sky filtering through white lace curtains.

No flicker from the bedroom fireplace.

Nothing.

Completely dark.

But the air was alive.

"I told you, I won't go if you want me to stay."

"And I told you, I don't like being put in this position," Pepper declared. "You set me up to be the villain. I don't like that, Tap Andrews."

"Now, darlin', I didn't mean to—"

"You're not going to 'now, darling' yourself out of this, Mr. Andrews. You asked me what I thought, and I told you. I don't like you going off chasin' a dozen lawless men by yourself."

"I won't be alone."

"You and an Indian you've never seen before today," she huffed.

"And his brother . . . and you're forgetting Lorenzo."

"No one has seen him since the wedding."

"Well . . . he and Selena can't stay in there forever."

"Sure they can. She can dance all night. She's thin."

"Anyway, there will be four of us. We'll just ride out, check the layout, and then—"

"You're going to try to capture that gang even if you find a hundred men. Don't you see, Tap? That's the way you are. You get something in your mind, and all the logic, all the tears, all the begging, all the threats in the world won't stop you."

A small, shrill voice wafted into the dark room from next door. "Will you two quit arguing and go to sleep. I need to get my rest!"

"Yes, Mother dear," Pepper called out.

Lying on his back, Tap turned toward Pepper, but he could see nothing but blackness. He took a big breath and let out an audible sigh.

After several moments of silence, Pepper spoke in almost a whisper. "What are you thinking about?"

"Well, you're right about me. That's the way I used to be. Pigheaded beyond good sense."

"Used to be?"

"I'm not goin' after that Yellow Sash bunch. Lady, you are much more important."

"I am?"

He reached over under the thick covers and laced his fingers in hers. "Yep. I'll tell Savage in the mornin'. It's probably doin' him a favor anyway. Word gets out he's stirrin' up trouble on this side of the river, and the whole tribe will have the devil to pay."

Pepper thought about rolling over and facing Tap but dismissed the idea for lack of strength. "Still . . . you did make a couple good points," she conceded.

"Oh?"

"Well, if—if there was a way to eliminate the Yellow Sash gang, the Millers could settle down on their farm, the tribe could relax on the reservation, and life on the Slash-Bar-4 could find some sort of normal pattern."

"Yeah, well . . . you were right too. It's not my business. They aren't threatenin' my family or my ranch. It's a job for the sheriff or U.S. Marshal."

"Of course," she continued, "*they* aren't going to do anything about it. One marshal isn't goin' to ride up there against twelve men. Besides, they think the Yellow Sash are scattered between the Yellowstone River and the Bighorn Mountains."

"That's true," Tap agreed. "But Dayton and that Yellow Sash bunch won't attack us. He's checked it out. He knows we've got too many guns, and besides, it would give away their position. I'll just sit back and let the authorities take care of it. That's why I resigned as sheriff in Cheyenne. That's why I left brand inspectin'. Someone else can take care of these kinds of things as well as I can. I can't settle ever' dispute and chase ever' *hombre malo*."

Pepper wanted to grasp Tap with her left hand, but could only reach halfway across her stomach. She settled for rubbing her toes along his long-john-covered leg. "This isn't just any dispute, of course," she offered. "The Millers are friends of ours, and it is on a neighboring place. If we don't do something, who will? Someone needs to stand up for what is right."

Tap slipped his left hand behind Pepper's neck and began to rub it with a strong, yet tender grip. "Darlin', I think I'm too scared to go up there tomorrow."

"Tap Andrews scared of twelve lawless men?"

"No, I'm not scared of them. I'm scared to leave you. What if you need me here? I can't take that chance."

"Let's be honest, Mr. Andrews. Let's suppose I started labor tonight. What would you do to help me?"

"Eh . . . I'd run get Mrs. Miller."

"Angelita can do that. Then what would you do?"

"I'd pace up and down out on the porch, I guess."

"Mr. Renten can do that."

"But what if there were complications? I could ride to town in the carriage and bring back a doc."

"Selena can do that."

"Well, I could . . . ," he stammered even as he continued to rub her neck, "I could pray for you."

Again Angelita's voice floated in muted tones into the room.

"This is the last time I'm telling you—if you don't settle down and go to sleep, there will be no dessert tomorrow. I need my sleep. I have to teach school in the morning."

"Yes, ma'am," Tap called out.

"You can pray for me while you ride up to the Pothook-H," Pepper whispered. "Besides, Lil' Tap won't be along for another couple of weeks."

"How do you know that?"

"Because I told the Lord I just couldn't take it anymore."

"What did He tell you?"

"To stop complaining."

"Really?"

"Well, that's my interpretation."

"Let me get this straight. You pitched a fit about me wanting to go up there, and now you're telling me to go?"

"Yes."

"Why did you change your mind?"

"I didn't. I thought you ought to go all along."

"But—you said—"

"I needed to know that you'd stay for me, Tap." She began to snif-fle. "I really, really needed to hear you say that. I can't explain it."

It was silent for a long time.

"Are you mad at me?" she finally whispered.

"Nope. How can I get mad at the purdiest gal in Montana?"

"I like it when the lights are out," she admitted.

"How come?"

"Because then I can pretend I'm thin again."

"Yeah," he laughed. "So can I."

"Forget it, cowboy!"

"Oh," he sulked, "I guess it's time for sleep?"

"Yes. We don't want to keep the teacher awake any longer."

A young voice rolled into the room. "Thank you!"

"Odessa, you've got five minutes to get dressed and be in the barn ready to go to work, or you're fired. . . . Do you hear me?" Tap hollered from the front porch of the cottage.

There was no answer.

He banged on the door with his clenched hand. "Lorenzo!" Someone shuffled about inside the cabin. Finally the door swung open several inches. Selena's coal-black hair billowed down to her waist over her shiny green satin robe. Her dark eyes sparkled. "Mr. Andrews! How nice to see you again."

Tap tipped his hat. "Mrs. Odessa, I need to talk to Lorenzo. We've got a job to do up in the mountains—that is, if you can spare him."

"My, that's a different tone than the screaming on the porch a few minutes ago."

"I just needed to get his attention."

"Well, something must have worked. He's been over in the barn since right before daybreak."

"He has?"

"Didn't you look there first?"

Tap shifted his weight from one foot to another and looked down at his boots. "Eh . . . no, ma'am. Look, I'm sorry for roustin' you out, Selena. It's just that . . ."

She reached out from the doorway and raised his chin with her hand until their eyes met. "Thanks again, Mr. Tapadera Andrews."

"Thanks?"

"For saving me again. You brought my Lorenzo to me and let us enjoy three days without interruption. Tell Pepper I'd like to call for a visit after a while."

Tap stepped back off the porch toward the barn. "I'll tell her. But, eh, don't wear anything that makes you look too skinny. She's gettin' mighty cantankerous about such things."

Tap noticed that another lodge was pitched in the pasture next to Jesse Savage's. *How do they do that? They move a whole family in and set up camp, and I don't hear a thing?*

When he reached the barn, Howdy was gathering up dishes from Jackson and Bean. Angelita was brushing down Queenie. Lorenzo Odessa was cinching the saddle of his red roan gelding.

"Look alive, boys. Here comes the old man," Lorenzo teased.

"Old man?" Tap replied. "You're four months older than me, and you know it."

"Now, now—you're the old man around here," Lorenzo insisted. "Isn't that right, Howdy?"

"Yep. Them's the rules. The one who lives in the big house and runs the place is the old man, no matter what his age."

Tap slapped Lorenzo on the back. "Speakin' of old men, you don't look any worse for wear. I presume married life is suitin' you fine."

"You know, Tap . . ." Odessa turned to look at Andrews. "What I can't figure is why in the world didn't you and me get married and settle down years ago?"

"We hadn't met the right ladies."

Lorenzo led his horse to the front of the barn and tied him to an iron ring. "Howdy says we have a few horse thieves to round up today. How many?"

"Just a dozen or so back-shooters, sneak thieves, bank robbers, and murderers."

Lorenzo winked at Angelita. "That won't take us all day, will it?"

"Two days. It takes a good eight hours to reach 'em."

"How many ridin' with us?"

"Two Indians."

"Can they fight?"

"They're friends with Wade Eagleman."

"So we got you, me, and two combative Indians goin' against twelve cutthroats. That don't hardly seem fair, does it?"

"No." Tap grinned. "I suppose one of us should stay at home."

"If you're lookin' for a volunteer to stay back . . . ," Lorenzo offered.

"Oh, no. I promised Selena I'd haul you out of here for a couple of days. She said she needed to clean the cottage and make sure the sun still comes up ever' day."

Lorenzo looked at Tap, then pushed his hat back and scratched his neck. "She's right."

"Besides," Tap continued, "these might be the boys that shot at you up on Cedar Mesa. How's your leg doing?"

"It hasn't bothered me for three, four days."

"That's because you haven't walked ten steps in that time."

"Yeah. Well, it's okay horseback anyway. When are we leavin'?"

"Have you had breakfast?"

"Yep. That Howdy Renten is the best cook north of Denver."

Tap raised his eyebrows and glanced over at Lorenzo.

"He's got to say that." Howdy spat tobacco to the dirt floor of the barn. "It's the rules. Never complain about the cook unless you want to run off to the privy sixteen times a day."

"Hey," Bean called out, "you can't just leave us here!"

"I'll take you to Billings when I get a chance," Tap assured him. "They'll probably lynch you when you get to town, so just enjoy yourself."

"I'm gettin' tired of being chained up to Jackson. He needs a bath. He stinks!" Bean protested.

"You ain't no rose," Jackson retorted. "I'm goin' to kill you, Andrews. I'll get loose, and I'll kill you."

Lorenzo strolled over to Bean and Jackson. "You know what I was thinkin', Tap? We ought to give these two old boys to the Indians. Just think of all the fun they could have usin' 'em for target practice."

"You cain't do that!" Bean protested. "It ain't—it ain't—"

"It ain't what?" Tap asked.

"It ain't . . . Christian!"

"Then we'll turn you over to Christian Indians," Lorenzo threatened.

Tap saddled up Roundhouse and led him out of the barn. Lorenzo followed with his horse. Handing the reins to Odessa, Tap stepped back into the barn. "Howdy, you look after things. If the sheriff shows up, give him Jackson and Bean."

"That posse might hang us without no trial," Bean hollered across the barn.

"A man ought to think about that before he sets out to rob a bank, shouldn't he?" Tap exhorted. Then he turned to Angelita. "Lil' darlin', you leave them ponies alone today. You're about to brush all the hair clean off them. Stick real close to Mama. She's goin' to need you."

"I will!" Angelita patted the colt on the head. "And if you happen to see Peter Miller, be sure and tell him . . ."

"Tell him what?" Tap asked.

"Eh, tell him he's already missed three days of school!"

With grub sacks and bedrolls fastened behind their cantles, Tap and Lorenzo rode out of the yard and around to the Indian lodges. Jesse Savage met them, leading a saddled buckskin stallion.

"Jesse, this is Lorenzo."

Savage tipped his flat-crowned, wide-brimmed hat and leaped to the saddle without putting a foot in the stirrup. Placing two fingers in his mouth, he let out a shrill whistle. "My brother is slow to get around. He just took a wife."

Tap glanced over at Lorenzo and shook his head.

Within a minute a short muscular Indian stepped out of the second tepee. He wore a long black frock coat over his buckskins. A silk top hat was cocked on his head, an eagle feather flagging straight up out of the hatband. He mounted his saddled pony on the off side with a leap, carrying a gun in his left hand.

"This is my brother, General Sheridan," Savage announced.

Tap pushed his hat back and cocked his head sideways. "General Sheridan Savage?"

"No," the top-hatted man replied. "My first name is General, and the last is Sheridan. I didn't like being called a savage, so I picked another name."

"Well, General, you picked a good one." Tap grinned. "Now I figure we'll ride up to Cedar Mesa and noon it there and then try to make it to the Pothook-H before dark. We'll scout things out and decide what to do."

"We can make it to their lodges in six hours," General Sheridan reported.

"How are we going to do that? We can't even get to Badger Canyon in six hours without runnin' the horses into the ground."

"There are other trails," Sheridan informed him. "And there are only eleven men in camp. The twelfth one was killed in a knife fight two days ago. They covered him over with rocks."

"How do you know that?" Tap asked.

"I have spent the last two days watching them."

Tap whistled. "Well, partner, you lead the way. Maybe somewhere along the trail we'll figure out how we're going to capture
this gang."

"Alive," Jesse Savage added. "We need to deliver them to the
authorities alive. Anything less, and they will declare it an Indian
massacre."

General Sheridan set out first on the trail to Cedar Mesa, carrying a converted .50-caliber Sharps carbine single-shot across his
lap. He seemed to be having a low-voiced ongoing conversation
with his horse the entire morning. Savage followed him on the
buckskin. He studied the ground for sign of game. Then came a
dozing Lorenzo Odessa, followed by Andrews with '73 Winchester
in hand and narrow brown eyes surveying the horizon.

The clouds were thick, gray, and drooping at treetop level.
There was little or no wind, and the recent rain kept the dust off
the trail. The temperature was coat-cool, and Tap's deerskin
gauntlets kept his hands warm.

They built a noon fire next to a lightning-struck pine on Cedar
Mesa and huddled around a coffeepot Jesse Savage had brought.

"Tap, you ever capture eleven men? I mean, alive?" Lorenzo
asked.

"Don't recall. How many was in that cattle rustler bunch last
spring?"

"Don't rightly remember, but we had more than four men after
them, and we turned them all over to Tom Slaughter. Guess we
can just hogtie 'em across their saddles like a pack string."

"There is an easier way," Jesse Savage suggested.

"Oh?" Tap swirled his coffee around in the bottom of his blue
tin cup.

"Get them to chase us back down out of the mountains and
then capture them. They will run down their horses in a dash of
overconfidence and be easy targets."

"I like the way this man makes plans," Odessa noted.

Tap gulped down his last swig of cold coffee and then fished
the grounds out of his teeth with his tongue. "Yeah, but that
bunches them up. We won't take the whole gang alive if we face
them all at once."

"That is true." Sheridan nodded. "Jesse's plan works only if we are planning to shoot them all." His wide smile revealed a silver tooth.

"You know, Tap, I'm kinda thinkin' it's a good thing these two are on our side." Lorenzo stood and tried to stretch out his sore left leg.

"Two will be easy to capture," General Sheridan reported. "They have two guards in the trees at the creek where the trail narrows before it reaches the broken barn. We can take those easily."

"They probably switch scouts at sundown. If we time it right, we can capture four of 'em before they know what's goin' on," Tap suggested.

"I like the way this man thinks," Sheridan mumbled.

Savage held the coffeepot out to the others and then poured out the remainder on the fire. "I'm glad he is on our side."

A distant rumble caused all four men to look toward the northeast. Tap reached for his rifle.

"It's a wagon," observed Savage.

"Just one horse," Odessa added.

"It's Miller's wagon." Tap stood up and peered toward the far horizon. "It's got to be. That's the only one up here . . . I think. We better see what's going on."

"We will stay here and break camp," Jesse Savage counseled. "It is one thing to be at the ranch—another to be seen up in the mountains."

Tap and Lorenzo mounted quickly and thundered across the mesa toward the careening farm wagon and the loping draft horse. As soon as the blond-haired boy driving the rig saw them approaching, he held up on the reins and jerked back on the hand brake.

Even before they reached the wagon, Peter Miller screamed, "Father's in the back, and he's hurt real bad."

"What happened?"

"They shot him. They shot him just like you said they would!" Peter cried out.

Tap pulled his canteen off his saddle horn and jumped to the ground, handing his reins to Odessa. He climbed up into the back of the wagon and rolled back a heavy green canvas tarp to reveal a badly bleeding Ezra Miller.

"How did it happen, Peter?"

"They took off after you last night, but at daybreak two of 'em rode right up onto our farm."

Ezra Miller's eyes were milky. Tap lifted the man's head and tried to help him take a drink.

"That one they call Sugar rode right up and said he was tired of waitin' for us to move and pulled his gun and shot Peaches in the head."

"Your other drivin' horse?"

"Yes, Father grabbed his whip and ran to chase Barley into the forest—this horse is named Barley—but the one with the sash shot Father in the chest!" Peter sobbed. "He said it was self-defense because Father was trying to beat him with the whip!"

Ezra Miller reached up and tugged at Tap's red bandanna. Andrews leaned close to the bearded man's mouth. "I should—I should—have listened to you, Andrews," Miller admitted. "We should have moved."

Tap poured a little water on the man's forehead. "Ezra, a man has to do what he can live with. Maybe you did do the right thing."

"The bullet went clear through him!" Peter cried out.

"We've got to get you to a doc, Ezra," Tap insisted.

Miller tried to shake his head. "Just—let me lay down and rest. I'm—I'm very tired."

"No. Peter needs to get you to a doctor. You've got to let him try. If you don't, it will haunt him the rest of his life. Do you understand what I'm sayin'?"

He slowly shook his head.

"Peter, me and Lorenzo are goin' after the men who shot your father. Can you make it to the ranch from here with one horse pulling this wagon?"

"Yes. It's mostly downhill."

"When you get to the ranch, have Mr. Renten hook up that new black carriage and the fast horses and race your father into Billings no matter what time of the night. Can you do it, son?"

"I think so." Tears streamed down his face.

"Your father's countin' on you, Peter."

"I can do it."

"I know you can," Tap assured him.

Ezra Miller reached up and grabbed Tap's bandanna and again pulled him close. "Don't kill him, Brother Andrews. Don't kill the man who shot me."

"Ezra, we'll try everything we can to bring him in alive. You have my word on that."

Miller nodded his head and then gasped for breath. "Tell him I forgive him," he mumbled.

Tap reached up and wiped a tear out of the corner of his eye. "I don't know if I can do that, Ezra."

"Please."

"I'll tell him . . . if I can."

"Good. That is good." With his eyes now closed, Miller tilted his head sideways. "And tell Lucinda that I have loved her pure and true."

"You tell her that in person, Brother Miller. Peter is goin' to get you to the ranch."

Tap jumped down from the wagon. "Take him to your Mama, son."

"I will, Mr. Andrews. I'll get him there." Peter slapped the reins against the big horse's rump.

Tap mounted up and watched the wagon rumble across the mesa.

"We really goin' to capture this Dayton character alive?" Lorenzo asked.

"Yep. I never lie to a dyin' man."

"You reckon he'll live to see his wife?"

"He'll make it. Love can keep a dead man alive for hours."

General Sheridan led them across the mesa and to the base of a steep, treeless granite mountain. Cascading off the rock, more than a hundred feet above them, was a two-foot-wide waterfall.

"We ain't goin' to try to ride over that mountain, are we?" Lorenzo questioned.

"We will ride through the mountain," Sheridan announced.

"We will ride up the Swift Death Canyon trail," Jesse Savage reported.

"I don't see no canyon trail," Odessa protested.

"Of course not. That's what makes it so valuable. There are two sources to that creek," General Sheridan explained. "One is that waterfall."

"And the other?" Tap questioned.

"A small stream from the upper valleys that has cut a trail right through the rock. It empties into the stream, and as long as the waterfall keeps flowing, it can't be seen. It will cut two hours off the journey to the Yellow Sash Gang."

"I figure I'll regret this," Lorenzo Odessa pressed, "but why is it called Swift Death Canyon?"

"Because it is just a narrow groove in the granite. If there is any rainfall at all in these mountains, the water becomes over twenty feet deep in a matter of seconds."

Tap watched the clouds hovering above them. "It looks like rain to me."

"You are right," Jesse Savage agreed.

"Then we better take the long route," Lorenzo declared.

"No. We will go up this canyon," Savage announced.

Lorenzo pulled off his drooping felt hat and scratched his sandy-blond hair. "But you just said it was goin' to rain!"

"No, I said that it looked like it was going to rain," Savage corrected. "It will not rain."

"Lead the way," Tap said. He purposely avoided looking Lorenzo in the eyes. *Lord, someday I'll be chasin' my last villain. I'm hopin' that it's because there are no outlaws left to chase. All I want to do is settle down with my Pepper-girl in my ranch house and raise beef cattle and babies. This is my last ride after bushwhackers. We clear these out, and I'll stay at home. No more ridin' at firin' guns. No more bustin' into buildin's with drunken gunmen tryin' to kill me. And no more Swift Death Canyons.*

A few drops of rain splashed off his face.

And no rain. Not for another half hour anyway. Please.

From time to time over the next four miles, it tried to rain. But they broke through the granite cliffs and entered the upper valley with the water no more than a foot deep. They emerged into what looked like a shallow lake, but General Sheridan turned them left and kept them hugging the granite slope until they reached dry land.

"That's quite a shortcut!" Tap called out.

General Sheridan held his finger to his lips and then turned in the saddle to whisper, "The guards are just down that trail."

"You mean this comes out right on top of them, and they don't know about it?" Lorenzo asked.

"This bunch is fortunate to find their way home from the saloon on a Saturday night," Jesse Savage scoffed.

The plan was simple.

Savage and Sheridan would sneak up on the guard on the east side of the trail. Tap and Lorenzo would take the one on the west side. They would coldcock, gag, and tie them, dragging them over toward the shallow lake. Then they would wait for the next shift and do the same. In the meantime, they would apprehend the two that had shot Ezra Miller as they returned to camp.

There were just two problems with the plan.

When they reached the trail, there were no guards posted.

And the moment Tap and Lorenzo rejoined Savage and Sheridan on the east side of the trail, fierce gunfire erupted, sending all four men diving into the rocks.

9

"hey don't know we're here? Someone knows we're here!" Lorenzo shouted. "So much for the element of surprise." Tap checked the lever on his rifle but stayed well hidden below the boulders. "Oh, I don't know. I was surprised!"

Flat on his stomach, Lorenzo Odessa crawled over to Tap and Jesse Savage. "I take it, they know about the Swift Death Canyon trail now."

General Sheridan scooted toward them, carrying the Sharps carbine across his shoulder. "It was probably my fault."

"What do you mean?" Savage asked his brother.

"When I was here before, they chased me down the trail a ways, but I thought I lost them before I reached the little lake. Perhaps they saw me cut back into the rocks at the top of the canyon."

"Perhaps? Looks like a sure thing to me," Lorenzo declared.

Scattered shots ricocheted off the granite, filling the air with rock chips and singing lead.

"Well, General Sheridan, this is a mighty poor time for you to remember that." Tap tried to look out east and see if the horses were still there.

"We goin' to hold out 'til dark and sneak out?" Lorenzo suggested.

"Nope. I figure it's time for a Crow deception."

Jesse Savage stared at Tap with unblinking dark eyes.

"We'll get 'em to chase us down the canyon and set an ambush at the other end," Tap announced.

"How do we know they'll all follow?" Lorenzo shouted above the roar of gunfire and a shower of granite chips.

"Because we look like easy pickin's. Ever'one wants to be in on a massacre."

"There are two problems with such a deception," Jesse Savage announced. "It is going to rain, and that canyon will be dangerous." A spray of granite chips blasted Savage's face, and he dove flat onto the ground.

"This isn't exactly a safe place." Tap rose up and fired two shots toward the woods.

"The other problem is that we have to make it to the horses," Savage announced from flat on the dirt.

"I'll go for the horses," Sheridan announced. "It's my fault we're in this."

"You can't bring them back here," Tap argued. "We'll all have to make a run for it."

"I ain't movin' too good on this bum leg," Odessa proclaimed.

"Jesse, you and the General go for the horses. Mount up and give us some cover. Then we'll catch up with you. Lorenzo, you take the left side. I'll take the right."

Savage glanced at his brother, and both men nodded. "When do we run?"

"Now!" Andrews and Odessa peeked out from behind the rocks and sent a barrage of 200-grain lead bullets toward the Yellow Sash gang's wooded position. After a dozen shots, Tap looked back. The Indians had made it to the horses. With the others safely out of range, Tap signaled Lorenzo to halt. Both men slumped back behind the rocks and crammed more cartridges into their breech-loading guns. Tap scooped up several brass casings from the dirt and shoved them into his coat pocket.

"What if them Indians just ride off and leave us here?" Lorenzo called out. "I don't hear them shootin'."

"They're gettin' to a closer position," Tap said.

"You got a lot of confidence in them."

"We don't have any choice, do we?"

"I reckon."

Odessa's answer was drowned out by the deafening blast of the 50-caliber Sharps, just behind them to the east.

"Come on, partner, that's our cue. Give me your arm," Tap called out.

Lorenzo carried his carbine in one hand and hung on to Tap's shoulder with the other as they crouched low and ran back across the trail toward the trees. Bullets buzzed like bees around them, but Tap never looked back. He dove for cover, then turned back to Odessa. "You take any lead, partner?"

"Nope? And you?"

"Not yet."

Odessa lay on his back and caught his breath. General Sheridan and Jesse Savage kept the barrage going.

"We're too old for this, Tapadera, bein' married men and all."

"You mean, we got too much to lose?"

"Yeah . . . somethin' like that." Lorenzo stared up at the clouds. "Is that drops of sweat, or is it beginning to sprinkle?"

"We better get to that canyon. Here comes the pride of the Crow Nation. Are you ready to mount?"

"Let's get out of here!" Lorenzo stood and waited as the horses were led up to them.

Tap shoved Lorenzo into his saddle. Then he mounted Roundhouse from the off side and spun him three times to the right.

"You mount Indian-style?" Sheridan asked.

"It's the only way he allows it."

"You want to sell that horse?"

"Yep."

"What do you want in trade?"

"I hate to interrupt you two in the middle of a big business deal," Odessa shouted, "but we're about to get ourselves killed!"

Jesse Savage grabbed the lead position, followed by Lorenzo Odessa, General Sheridan, and then Tap Andrews. The scattered pines offered good cover from the Yellow Sash bunch. Tap could hear the now-mounted pursuers thundering after them.

"We'll be exposing ourselves when we ride at the edge of the lake and the canyon wall," Lorenzo called back.

"I'll cover you three," Tap hollered. "Then one of you drop back and cover for me."

"Are we still trying to take them all alive?" Sheridan called out.

"At the moment, we're just trying to get out of here alive ourselves! Now go on!"

While raindrops splashed the waters of the shallow lake, Tap fired round after round from the saddle. All three ahead of him found the canyon entrance. When he heard the .50-caliber Sharps echo like a small cannon out of the rock, he spurred Roundhouse out from behind the trees.

Halfway to the canyon entrance Tap felt something stab him like a knife in the calf of his left leg. He continued to spur Roundhouse but glanced down to see blood drip into the water.

I don't know if it's me or Roundy that's losin' blood!

"Come on, boy, we're goin' to make it. Don't slow down on me!"

The big gray gelding plowed through the water and reached the rocks where General Sheridan fired his 50-caliber bullets. Tap signaled for him to go on down the canyon. In the protection of the natural rock shield at the mouth of the narrow, twisting canyon, Tap examined his wound. Taking off his red bandanna, he shoved it up his canvas ducking pants leg to stop the blood that had started to puddle up in his boot.

He peered over the rocks and fired two shots at the pursuers, who were now starting down the submerged gravel ledge at the edge of the canyon wall.

Tap bent to the left and ran his now-ungloved left hand along the fender of the saddle until he found a bullet hole in the leather.

"Where are you hit, Roundy? Maybe me and the saddle slowed that bullet down a little."

He drew a bead on the lead rider pursuing them and then remembered his promise to Ezra Miller. "Mister, you'll get to live another day." Tap shot into the rock cliff next to the man. The horse jumped to the left into the deeper water of the little lake.

Bending down again, Tap eased his hand along Roundhouse's left side until his middle finger found blood oozing from the horse's flank. Keeping his eye on the trail where the Yellow Sash gang was cautiously approaching, he stuck his finger into the bullet hole in the horse. Tap's finger hit the still-warm lead bullet about three-quarters of an inch into the horse's flesh.

"Hang on, boy!"

Tap spun the gelding to the left in the two-foot-deep water and jammed another finger into the bullet hole. Clutching the lead between his fingers, he yanked the bullet out, dropping it into the water.

Roundhouse bucked hard, exposing Tap's position. Several shots rang out around him. With his blood-smeared left hand, he jerked out his shirttail and ripped off a six-inch piece. Then he bent low and poked some of the cloth into the horse's bullet hole and pushed the leather fender against the wound to hold the cloth in place.

"Let's get out of here, Roundy. It's really starting to rain!"

The water in the three-foot-wide canyon was rising with every turn in the trail. Occasional bullets ricocheted toward him, but he was staying out of sight of his attackers.

Soon water lapped at the heels of his boots. Rain soaked his coat and the tops of his duckings. He began to experience symptoms of shock from the bullet wound. Sweat burst out on his forehead, even as the hard-driving rain diluted it and washed it away.

Lord, this canyon is going to flood. It's just a matter of when. I'd rather be out of here before it does. I figure that's exactly what old Noah told You too.

"Come on', Roundy, you can do it. Stretch those long, old legs of yours. . . . Come on, boy, heyaah!"

Tap spurred repeatedly as the gelding slipped, slid, and stumbled through the deep water on the trail. He could not see any of the others up ahead. Continuing the twisting descent, Tap shoved his rifle back into the scabbard and pulled his Colt revolver. When a bullet ricocheted in the rocks high above his head, he turned and squeezed off a round, even though no one was in sight.

Tap's boots were almost submerged in the water, and Roundhouse sloshed along with his head up and his ears back. Even though Tap figured that it wasn't much past midafternoon, the little bit of sky above the steep canyon walls was so dark he could see no more than twenty yards ahead.

He wiped his face with the sleeve of the rain-soaked canvas jacket and finally shoved his revolver back into his holster. The rain saturated his duckings and was running down his leg, flooding his wound, causing it to burn like a succession of yellow jacket stings.

The canyon still towered above and in front of them, seeming to stretch longer than the ascent. Tap fought the urge to stop and bandage his leg with a dry sack he knew was in his saddlebags.

I don't need to be chasin' these boys, and I don't need them chasin' me. I don't need to be shot . . . and I sure don't need to drown in this godforsaken canyon.

Okay . . . You haven't forsaken it. But surely it doesn't occupy the central part of Your mind very often. Except for right now . . . I hope.

The rising water slowed Roundhouse down to a fast walk. Tap knew that if the water raised another foot, the horse would have to swim.

The water is coming up slower than I thought it would. The Indians said it comes down like a wall. . . . If a wall of water flushes through here now, there's no way to survive. It would be like that old Egyptian army caught in the Red Sea. Well, I'm not Moses or a child of Abraham . . . by birth—at least, I don't think I am—but, Lord, I surely would like to make it to the other side!

Ahead in the narrow, shadowy gorge, Tap thought he could see the waterfall that marked the end of the canyon. With his boots now filled with water, he spurred the frightened gelding who was jumping and swimming as rocks and boulders tumbled under the water and beneath his hooves. A deafening roar echoed down the canyon behind him, and he knew the wall of water must be coming.

Lord, I know I ought to be prayin' for the men back there too. But I just don't know what to say. . . . I'm not as full of grace and wisdom as Ezra Miller. . . . Thy will be done.

The water broke out of the canyon with such force that it shoved Tap and Roundhouse right into the backside of the waterfall, which now dropped rocks and debris as well as water. Tap leaned over and grasped Roundhouse's neck as they got completely drenched in the cascade.

The gray gelding hit the rocky creek on the other side of the waterfall, swimming toward shore. Tap lay across the saddle horn holding the horse's neck. When they finally reached shallow water, Tap reined up to glance back at the canyon entrance.

He heard the roar of the Sharps above the thunder of the water. General Sheridan, Savage, and Odessa signaled him from a bluff about a quarter of a mile to the east. He spurred the reluctant Roundhouse until he reached them.

"You take a bullet?" Odessa pointed at his blood-soaked pant leg.

"Me and Roundy both. I pulled the bullet out of him, but we both lost some blood."

"We thought you'd drown. How did you make it out of there?" Savage questioned.

"We held our breath and said our prayers," Tap replied.

"The horse is worth less if he is shot," Sheridan announced.

"I wouldn't sell ol' Roundy now for a thousand dollars in gold!" Tap handed the reins to Lorenzo and slipped to the ground, keeping his weight off his left leg.

"Here it comes!" Jesse Savage shouted above the roar of water in the canyon.

Boulders the size of milk buckets, along with horses and outlaws, washed out with a twelve-foot wall of water that blasted through the waterfall and instantly flooded everything below the cliff. A good-sized lake formed at the canyon entrance. All four men stared at the sight in silence. Within minutes the water coming out of the canyon receded to a depth of about five feet, and the instant lake began to drain back into the creekbed.

"Do we go out there and count bodies?" Lorenzo asked.

"Well . . . we didn't shoot 'em," Tap commented. "They can't blame us or the Crow Nation for this. But we better haul in the bodies to prove that point."

"I think some are alive," General Sheridan reported.

Tap took out his boot knife and sliced his pant leg up to his knee. Then he pulled the dry cotton sack out of his saddlebags and tied it around his calf. The rain continued to roll off the back brim of his felt hat onto an already soaked coat.

"You up to this?" Lorenzo called out.

Tap grabbed the saddle horn with two hands, pulled himself halfway up the side of the prancing horse, and then shoved his right foot into the stirrup and yanked his left leg over the saddle.

"You ain't in any shape to mount and dismount," Lorenzo cautioned.

"Neither are you, Odessa. You go round up any horses left alive and put the wounded ones down. We'll pull saddles later. Me and the boys will check on the men."

It stopped raining right before dark. By then they had a roaring fire blazing on top of the bluff at the northern edge of Cedar Mesa. Laid out under the cedars, with saddle blankets covering their heads, were four dead members of the Yellow Sash gang. Five other water-soaked men sat in the mud, tied back to back, with the flames of the fire revealing tired and dejected faces.

Tap's crew sat on saddles closer to the fire, steam rising off their soaked clothing. General Sheridan examined his hat, which now sported only half of an eagle feather. Tap's left foot was propped up on a saddle. He held a steaming coffee cup in his hand, warming his fingers and face.

"We could use some of that coffee, mister!" one of the bound men hollered.

"You got a cup, or do you want me to jist pour it straight into your mouths?" Odessa growled.

"We ain't got no cups!"

"Then you'll have to wait until we're through with ours. These boys should have rode down to Arizona. It's pretty warm at this time of year, ain't it, Tap?"

"I don't know, Odessa. Arizona's no place for amateurs. . . . Boys, we got some coffee and beans left. Now you'll have to share the same plates and cups. Only I need to know if Sugar Dayton and the other hombre rode into the canyon with you, or did they stay home and let you do the dirty work?"

"We ain't tellin' you nothin'!" one man shouted.

"Then it will be a long, cold night," Odessa called back.

Jesse Savage squatted down to inspect Tap's wound. He was holding a green tin box. "You need a little of this." He pried open the lid.

"It looks like wagon axle grease."

"It's an old Indian remedy. It keeps the wound from getting gangrene."

"What's in it?"

"How would I know?" Savage grinned. "I bought it at a pharmacy in Denver. But it works. Burns like a red-hot horseshoe, but it works."

Tap bit down on one of his water-soaked leather gauntlets as Jesse Savage applied the thick ointment to his calf and rewrapped the towel around it. Gasping for breath, Tap dropped the glove. "I hate it when the cure hurts worse than the injury."

General Sheridan squatted between Tap and Savage. "We've got nine men and eight horses accounted for. Five men and four horses are alive."

"Are you sure we don't have Dayton?" Lorenzo quizzed.

"I know Dayton," Savage insisted. "He's not here."

"If he didn't come with the others, maybe he swung around the mountain to flank us," Tap suggested.

"Which means he and another could be ridin' across the mesa right about now!" Lorenzo stood up. "You want me to douse the fire?"

"Nope. Build it up. We want to make sure they can see it." Tap turned to Savage and Sheridan. "Jesse, you and the General help me see that these boys get a little closer to the fire. In fact, we can let them have all the fire. We'll just sit back in the shadows and see who comes to visit."

Sheridan turned to his brother. "I like the way this man thinks!"

"But we don't shoot them," Tap cautioned. "At least, not if we can help it. I aim to keep that promise I made Ezra."

Within minutes the five bound men had been dragged to the fire, filled with a few sips of steaming coffee, and then gagged. Some sat and stared at the flames. Others lay down, allowing the heat to dry out their soaked clothes.

Expecting riders from the east, Tap and Lorenzo hid in a short clump of cedars to the south. The Crow brothers waited in the lava rocks on the north. Clouds started to blow east. A cold, star-lit night unfolded. Even though they were gloved, Lorenzo blew into his cupped hands. "This is what I can't figure—we won the battle, and we're out here freezin'. They lost, and they're curled up asleep next to the fire."

"Four of 'em are dead."

"That's a good point," Lorenzo conceded.

The distant crackle of the fire and soft moan of the wind in the trees were the only sounds for several minutes.

"Tap, what do you reckon ol' Savage and Sheridan are talkin' about?"

"About how nice it would feel to be back in their own tepees scooched up to the missus."

"You think so?"

"There ain't all that much difference between whites and Indians," Tap observed.

Both men stared at the distant fire. Lorenzo coughed. Tap held his finger to his lips. Both turned as they heard a steady muted sound out on the mesa. Tap strained to see in the starlit, moon-less darkness. *It's too muddy for sticks to break or hooves to rattle the rocks.* He heard the click of Lorenzo's revolver cock. He pulled his own gun from the still slightly wet Mexican loop hol-ster.

Two men rode horses into the clearing between their position and that of Sheridan and Savage. Tap could see the red glow of a quirley. He thought he heard the men mumble something. The one with the cigarette was waving his arms, and the other turned toward the Indian brothers.

Come on, Dayton . . . come on. Circle around the fire and check out your buddies before you hello your way in. Come on. This is mighty nice of you.

The rider coming their way stayed in the darkness of the trees and rode within three or four feet of them. He stopped, turned his horse toward the fire, stood in the stirrups, and leaned forward as he stared at the scene.

Lorenzo lung   f rward in the night and grabbed the man's vest, jerking the   /   ied rider right out of the saddle.

"What the—

The barrel o   s Colt creased the man's hat before he hit the mud. He didn'   e. Tap grabbed the reins of the prancing horse while Lorenzo   t his gun pointed at the downed man. Both stared in the   /   :ion of the Indians. Finally they heard a soft, lonely magpi   y

"That's th   s gnal," Tap said.

Lorenzo   :k two fingers between his lips and let out a piercing whistle   t woke up the men around the fire. Jesse Savage came out o   he shadows leading a horse with a man lying cold-cocked ac   ie saddle. General Sheridan followed.

Tap sp   t the Indians. "Mighty nice of these guys to split up like that.

"It w   uch of a challenge." Savage grinned.

"Whi   n   is Dayton?" Tap asked.

"Yo   avage reported.

All t   nd men were sitting up straight around the fire.

"W   ky here, boys," Lorenzo chided. "The king of the Yello   S s   outfit, Sugar Dayton, has come to rescue you. Ain't that   e   nim and this other fella? I'm sure you'll want to thank 'em   h never they wake up. They seem to be takin' a nap right nov

   e   t :d up the two unconscious men and pulled down the ga   c   ie other five. Then they tossed more wood on the fire ar   s e hed out their bedrolls. Tap took the first guard duty. A c   ours later, General Sheridan took the second.

  .p iad barely fallen asleep under the now cloudless, cold night   y w en the stocky Indian tapped his shoulder. Tap peered into   w le brown face topped with the silk hat.

   A wagon's coming across the prairie!" Sheridan announced.

Ta p sat up and jammed on his hat. "A wagon? . . . I don't hear   ' The rattle of a sideboard and the creak of poorly greased   he ls filtered across the mesa.

Sheridan held up his right index finger. "One horse."

"Peter? The boy that was on the mesa this afternoon?"

"Perhaps."

"Who else would bring a wagon out here? Wake up your brother and Lorenzo. I'll build up the fire. I don't want him to miss us."

"We'll hide back in the trees. Perhaps you are wrong," Sheridan proposed.

Tap nodded and stuffed sticks of mostly dry wood on the embers of the fire. Lorenzo rubbed his eyes and pulled on his hat and boots.

"You figure it's young Miller?" he asked Tap.

"We'll soon find out."

They couldn't see the wagon yet, but it was getting closer. Tap stood between the fire and the approaching wagon.

"You goin' to strut around in plain sight?" Lorenzo questioned.

The wagon stopped just out of the light of the fire.

"Peter, is that you?" Tap yelled.

"Yeah. Is that you, Mr. Andrews?" a young voice hollered.

"Drive it on in, son. Ever'thing's fine. We caught 'em all."

The big draft horse plodded into view pulling the farm wagon and a blanket-wrapped Peter Miller.

"Come on down and warm up," Tap offered.

Peter jumped to the ground. Somehow he looked a little taller than Tap remembered.

"Father died, Mr. Andrews. He died in Mama's arms," Peter sobbed.

"Did they get to talk?"

"For a few minutes."

Tap wiped tears out of his own eyes. "I hurt all over for you. I'm glad he got to see your mama. Peter, gettin' your daddy home to her was the best gift you could have given them. I'm proud of you."

Peter motioned to the four men lying with saddle blankets over their heads. "Are they dead?"

"Yep."

"Did you kill 'em?"

"Nope. They drowned," Tap reported.

"Drowned?"

"We had a little flash flood in the canyon."

"Is Dayton dead?"

Tap stared at the flames and then looked into Peter Miller's eyes. "Eh, no, son. Ol' Sugar ran into a pistol barrel and is sleepin' kind of peaceful."

"Where?"

"The second man over there." Tap pointed. Savage and Sheridan stole back toward the fire.

Peter Miller stalked up to Dayton and kicked his boots. "Wake up!" he hollered.

Sugar Dayton blinked his eyes and squinted at Peter.

"You killed my papa," Peter screamed.

Dayton searched the flickering shadows until he spied Tap. "Get this kid away from me!"

"You killed my father, and he didn't even have a gun!" Peter cried.

"I should've shot you too!" Dayton growled. He turned to Tap. "Are you Andrews? I said, get this kid away from me!"

"You murdered the boy's father right in front of his eyes. The only reason I didn't shoot you," Tap replied, "is because I promised Ezra Miller I wouldn't. It's beyond my wisdom to know why God in heaven allows some worthless dung pile like you to stay alive and a good man like Peter's father to die. But I don't argue with the Almighty. So don't be tellin' me what I should and shouldn't do!"

"Give me a gun!" Peter cried out.

"Why?"

"I'm going to kill him!"

"I promised your daddy that—"

"Well, I didn't promise him!" Peter yelled. "Give me a gun!" The young boy's tear-filled eyes went from Tap to Odessa and finally to Savage and Sheridan. "Indians? Are they the ones with tepees at the ranch?"

"They're friends of mine."

"Give me a gun!"

"Get this kid away from me!" Dayton hollered.

Andrews pulled out his Colt .44 revolver and handed it, grip first, to the boy.

"Mister, you cain't let that boy shoot me!"

"Sure I can."

"But I'm unarmed!"

"So was his father."

The bound man frantically jerked at the leather straps that lashed his hands and feet.

Peter Miller stared at the gun in his hand. "How does it work?"

"Well, you just pull back that hammer all the way, point it at what you want to hit, and pull the trigger."

"Mister, I don't like this game," Sugar Dayton screamed. "You got to take me to jail! I get a fair trial! It's my right!"

Tap turned to Lorenzo. "Did you ever hear of anyone who wanted to go to jail so bad?"

Peter Miller used both hands and pulled back the trigger until it clicked. Then he turned to the bound man.

"He's goin' to kill me!" Dayton yelled.

"Where do I aim?" Peter asked.

"If you shoot him in the head, he'll be dead the minute you pull the trigger. If you shoot him in the gut, he could live in agony for a day or two before he died."

Peter pointed the gun toward the man's midsection.

"Wait!" Dayton screamed. "I've got money. Stop him, Andrews. I'll tell you where there's money—lots of it!"

"How much money?" Tap asked.

"Two thousand dollars from the Billings bank job. How about it?"

"That's not enough."

"Wait! I've got more. You can have it all! Maybe five thousand all together. Up at the headquarters. In a tin box behind the loose boards next to the stove. Now call him off!"

"Dayton, that's kind of you to tell us where the money is, but if Peter shoots you or not, it will be his own decision."

"You cain't do this! You've got to stop this. This is cold-blooded murder!"

"You saying that you're against murder?"

"When I'm the one gettin' murdered, I am!"

Peter lifted the gun and again pointed it toward the bound man.

"Now he is right about one thing, Peter. It is murder to shoot an unarmed, bound man."

"I don't care," Peter sniffled. "He killed my father!"

"Before you pull that trigger, let me tell you what your father told me. Our last conversation—he said for me to tell this man that he forgave him."

"He said that?" Peter gasped.

"Yep. Right there in the back of your wagon. You see, he didn't want to go meet his Maker with an unforgiving heart. Peter, I've been shot half a dozen times, including today, and never in my life have I forgiven the man or woman who did it. I just don't have it in me. Your father was quite a man."

"I'm going to kill him anyway!"

"Well . . . if you do, you'll have to pull that hammer back another click. You just have it on safety right now."

"Tap," Lorenzo protested, "do you know what you're doin'?"

"I hope so."

Peter used both thumbs and pulled the hammer back until it clicked a second time.

"Oh, no, no," Dayton moaned.

"Peter, do you believe in heaven?" Tap asked.

"Yeah. But he's not going there!"

"Nope, I don't reckon he is. But is your daddy there?"

"Yes."

"Do you think he can see what's goin' on now?"

"I don't know."

"Well, let's suppose he can. What do you think he'd want you to do."

"But I've got to do it!" Peter sobbed. "He killed my father."

"We all know he killed your father. The Lord knows he killed your father. But you can't do it, Peter. It will ruin your life."

"Killing men didn't ruin yours."

"It didn't exactly make mine wonderful. Besides, I've never in my life shot a man who wasn't shootin' at me or someone else first. Hand me the gun now. Make your father happy."

"I can't. I've got to kill Dayton!"

"Any fool can pull the trigger. Look at these men. . . . Look at 'em, Peter!" Tap urged. "If they were in your shoes, ever'one of them would pull the trigger. You mean to tell me that Ezra and Lucinda Miller didn't raise their boy any better than these back-shooters and cattle rustlers? Let's see what you're really made of. It's your day to become a man, son—to become the kind of man that would make your mama and daddy proud. Hand me the gun."

"Listen to him, boy. Listen to him!" Dayton called.

Tap grabbed the man by the coat collar, almost lifting him off the ground. "Dayton, if I hear another word out of you, I'll shoot you myself. Is that clear?" He shoved the man back to the ground so hard that he fell over on his side.

"Peter?"

Young Miller lowered the gun to his side. "They'll think I'm a coward if I don't pull the trigger."

"Who?" Tap quizzed.

Peter looked around at Lorenzo, then at the Indians. "How about them?" Peter waved the gun at the other bound men who had been watching the whole proceedings. Most of them tried to dive out of the aim of the cocked revolver.

"Who cares what they think? A good reputation lies only in the minds of honorable men. Give me the gun. You proved that you could have done it . . . if you wanted to."

Peter Miller gazed up at the star-filled sky. "Daddy, I wanted to shoot him for your sake . . . and now I'm not shooting him—for your sake. I sure hope you understand!"

He gave the gun back to Tap.

Daylight was breaking behind them as they paraded out of the trees of the Bull Mountains and onto the sloping prairie of the Yellowstone River drainage. A cool, stiff wind blew into their faces from the west. Tap gazed at a distant column of smoke from the ranch headquarters.

Well, someone's stoked the fire.

Tap led the procession on Roundhouse. Peter Miller rode

Odessa's roan behind him. Then the Miller wagon, driven by Lorenzo, lumbered along, loaded with eleven members of the Yellow Sash gang—four deceased. Their leader, Sugar Dayton, sulked at the front of the wagon. And trailing last were Jesse Savage and General Sheridan leading six saddled horses.

"You see that rider, Tap?" Lorenzo hollered from the wagon.

Andrews strained to survey the distant horizon. "Where?"

"I do believe the old man needs eyeglasses. Peter, ride up there and show him."

Peter Miller kicked the roan and trotted alongside Roundhouse. "Look straight at the barn. . . . See that draw? A rider will come over that berm," Peter instructed.

Tap rode at a fast walk and waited for the rider to appear. *I don't need eyeglasses. It's just that there is so much mud he isn't kickin' up dust.*

"It looks like a black horse," Peter added.

"It does, huh?" Tap murmured. "It's probably Onespot. Angelita must be out for a ride."

"At daybreak?" Peter asked.

"She's been mighty worried about you."

"She has?"

"Yep, but don't you dare tell her I said that."

"Well, it's not her. It looks like Mr. Renten."

Tap turned back to the wagon. "I'll ride up and see what's goin' on. You come in at your own pace," he yelled to Odessa.

Roundhouse was ready to romp. Within seconds they were galloping up to the oncoming rider. Tap reined up, and the big gray gelding shut it right down as they drew even with Howdy Renten on Onespot.

"What's up, partner?"

Renten waved toward the distant wagon. "You bringin' in that gang?"

"Yep."

"They all alive?"

"Nope. Four drowned."

"Drowned, you say?"

"What's happening at the ranch?"

"Sheriff and a dozen-man posse showed up this mornin'."

"Did you give them Jackson and Bean?"

"Yep, but the sheriff didn't want to leave without talkin' to you. That's why I rode out."

"What's he want to talk about?"

"Jackson and Bean told him that you took the two thousand dollars."

"And he believed them?"

"All I know is that we've got a posse parked in the yard."

"How's Pepper?"

"I ain't heard nothin', so I reckon she's just as plump and purdy as ever."

"I'll ride in and talk to the sheriff. I'm glad he's here. Keeps me from havin' to take a trip to town."

With most of the ranch buildings puffing smoke from their chimneys, two Indian lodges in the pasture, and a dozen men milling around the yard, the Slash-Bar-4 looked like a mountain town on the Fourth of July.

The sheriff was waiting for Tap at the gate when he rode up. The lawman held it open while Tap and Howdy passed through.

"Good to see you, Sheriff."

"Andrews, Jackson and Bean said you took the bank money off them."

"Yeah, and they told me you were a yella, monkey-faced coward. But I don't believe a word they say. Do you?" Tap challenged.

The flustered sheriff pushed his hat back and muttered, "That ain't the point. Did you take the money?"

"Nope. But I can tell you exactly where it is. After you take these two, Sugar Dayton, and the entire Yellow Sash gang into town, you can ride out to the Pothook-H and pick up the bank money and a whole lot more."

"The Yellow Sash gang alive?"

"Four of 'em drowned."

"Drowned?"

"Am I pronouncin' that word wrong? 'Cause ever'body keeps repeatin' it. The money's out at the old Pothook-H headquarters." Tap dismounted carefully, keeping his weight on his right foot.

"You shot?" the sheriff asked.

"I think that's obvious."

Suddenly Angelita rushed across the yard barefoot. She held her long nightgown high. "Hurry!" she screamed. "Mama's gone into labor. Hurry! I'll get Mrs. Miller!"

Tap limped toward the house.

"Andrews! What about that money?"

"Lorenzo will tell you when he gets here!" Tap shouted. "Wait for the wagon."

"What about those Indians? It's illegal for them to be on this side of the river!"

Tap turned back to the man with the badge. The others in the posse were scattered within hearing distance. "They're friends of mine. They came to help me celebrate the birth of my child. It's all right, Sheriff. They have permission from General Sheridan."

"They do? You know General Sheridan?"

"We're good friends," Tap assured the lawman. Then he hobbled to the front door.

Pepper had begun labor, but it soon became evident it wasn't going to be a quick birth. There were periods of pain followed by long stretches of rest.

Tap stayed in the room with her, Mrs. Miller, and Selena. Angelita spent her time giving progress reports to Howdy and Lorenzo, who waited on the front steps of the big house; the Miller children, who played on the porch of the bunkhouse; the Crow families, who huddled around a campfire at the tepees; and the posse and outlaws, who camped near the barn.

After a couple of hours the pains intensified and came more quickly. But Pepper was determined not to cry out.

But the moment soon came when that resolution faltered. She lay in the middle of her bed, her flannel gown unbuttoned at the neck, sweat beading her forehead.

"It won't be long, darlin'. You're doin' fine," Tap told her again and again.

"Fine?" she roared. "I'm being torn in two, and you say I'm doin' fine!"

"Ever'thing will turn out mighty good. You just relax."

"Relax? I've got a fifty-pound baby in here trying to get out, and you tell me to relax!"

"You don't have to shout, darlin'. I'm right here."

The sharp pain that shot through her body was so great Pepper didn't even know she screamed, but by the way everyone in the room jumped, she saw it must have been a loud one. Tears poured down her cheeks as her eyes searched the room for Tap.

"Shoot me!" she pleaded.

"What?"

"If you love me, you'll shoot me and put me out of this misery!"

"Now, darlin', don't you be—"

"Are you goin' to shoot me or not?" she hollered.

"Of course not!"

"Give me a gun, and I'll do it myself!"

"Nope."

"Well, don't just stand there gawking at me. Go do something!" she screamed.

Tap looked helplessly at Selena and Lucinda Miller. Mrs. Miller spoke in a low voice. "Mr. Andrews, why don't you go down and make us all a hot cup of tea?" Then she lifted her eyebrows. "And please . . . take your time."

"What? Oh . . . okay, I'll go. Let me know if anything—I mean—"

"You'll be the first to know, Brother Andrews," Lucinda Miller replied.

Tap thought about going back upstairs to be with Pepper.

He considered going outside and sitting on the porch with Lorenzo and Howdy.

He ended up limping back and forth in the living room, an empty coffee cup in his hand.

Now, Lord, I know I've been prayin' a lot lately. And I hate to be botherin' You all the time. But there was a whole bunch of years I never said much to You at all. So maybe I'm just tryin' to catch up. But this time . . . well, if I only get so many answers to prayer in my lifetime, I'd like to cash 'em in right now. Give

Pepper the strength she needs to bring that baby into this world and give the little one a healthy body. You just have to make sure ever'thing's all right!

Tap winced and paused at the bottom of the stairs every time he heard Pepper cry out.

Lord, it's me again. I've been thinkin', and I guess I don't know how to pray. I know what my heart wants. But I don't know what Your heart wants. You're in charge. Just get me ready for whatever comes next.

Tap gaped out the window at the ranch yard. From the porch to the bunkhouse, to the barn and corrals, to the tepees—dozens of pairs of eyes seemed to be staring back at him. He took a sip from his cup and never noticed it was empty.

Pepper's long scream brought him back to the base of the stairs. A baby's cry sounded through the house. He hobbled up the stairs.

"It's a boy!" Angelita shouted as she ran out to the top of the stairs. "Tell everyone it's a boy!"

Stunned, Tap turned to face the front door as it flew open. Both Lorenzo and Howdy rushed in.

"Well?" Lorenzo queried.

"It's a . . . boy," Tap mumbled.

He could hear Howdy scream across the yard, "It's a boy!" Howdy and Lorenzo scurried out. Tap heard the roar of the Sharps .50-caliber fired in celebration. But Tap Andrews couldn't move. He sucked air and wiped the corners of his eyes. The sound of Angelita running out to the top of the stairs again caused him to turn back around.

"And it's a girl!" she shouted "Really. A cute little girl!"

"You said it was a boy!"

"A boy and a girl—that's called twins, you know!"

"Twins? But . . . how—how can she do that?" Tap stuttered.

"Well, when I have time, I'll try to explain it to you. Now go tell the others, and when you get back, things will be cleaned up enough to come up and see your family."

"Twins!"

"Oh, for heaven's sake." Angelita sighed. "I'll go tell them myself. But you can't go in there until they call you."

She scampered past him on the stairs.

Tap thought he stood on the stairs for an hour.

Only eight minutes later Mrs. Miller hiked out of the room carrying a porcelain basin stacked with soiled sheets and wadded-up towels.

"You may come in, Brother Andrews. It looks like they are all quite healthy."

Selena met him at the doorway. She stood on her tiptoes and kissed his cheek. "Congratulations, Daddy! We'll wait out here. She's pretty exhausted, so don't plan to stay too long."

Pepper lay in the middle of the bed on her back. Blanket-wrapped and cradled in her left arm was a tiny person with a sweet red face, eyes pinched shut, and a shock of dark hair jutting out from under the wrap. In her right arm lay another round-faced darling with closed eyes and a little pink bald head.

Pepper's eyes were bloodshot.

Her hair was matted against her head.

Her lips were chapped, almost white, except for a little blood on the lower one.

But she showed a wide, dimpled smile. "They're perfect, Tap. I looked them all over, and they're perfect!" She started to sob.

"You done good, Mrs. Andrews. You done really good." Tap stared down at the two sleeping little ones. "Those have got to be the prettiest babies ever born on this earth."

"I believe you're right, Mr. Andrews. Did I actually ask you to shoot me?"

"Yep."

"I'm very glad you didn't."

"So am I." He felt as if his jaw was locked in a permanent grin. "How you feelin', darlin'?"

Pepper stared first at the baby in her right arm and then at the one in her left. She looked Tap right in the eyes. "I feel . . . skinny!"

Then she puckered her parched lips for a kiss.

APPENDIX

AIMEE "PEPPER" PAIGE ANDREWS

b. 1852, Atlanta, Georgia;
m. December 24, 1882;
d. 1933, Yellowstone County, Montana.

TAPADERA ANDREWS

b. 1855, Tuolumne County, California;
d. 1921, Yellowstone County, Montana.

THEIR CHILDREN:

(All born in Yellowstone County, Montana)

ZACHARIAH HATCHER ANDREWS

b. 1883;
m. Martha Naomi Clark, December 24, 1903;
d. 1959
They had 7 children, 21 grandchildren,
47 great-grandchildren.

SUZANNE CEDAR ANDREWS

b. 1883;
m. Paul James Stoner, December 24, 1903;
d. 1976
They had 5 children, 10 grandchildren,
32 great-grandchildren.

PATRICIA PAIGE ANDREWS

b. 1885;
d. 1892
"Punkin'" died from cholera and
went to be with her Jesus on Easter Sunday.

EUGENE STUART ANDREWS
b. 1887;
m. Elizabeth May Brannon, December 24, 1919;
d. 1961
She died in an automobile accident in 1921.
They had no children. Eugene never remarried.

TAPADERA ANDREWS, JR.
b. 1895;
m. French actress Lea Devrais, December 24, 1925;
d. 1974.
They had 3 children, 7 grandchildren,
2 great-grandchildren (as of this printing).

The Slash-Bar-4 is now run by Tapadera Andrews, IV,
and his wife, Mary Beth Andrews (nee Riggins).

Two years after the death of her husband,
Lucinda Miller married Henry "Stack" Lowery.

In 1893 Peter Miller Lowery married Angelita Rachel Gomez.
They inherited the Sphinx gold mine in 1899. Still in limited pro-
duction, the mine is totally owned today by the Lowery family.
Angelita died in 1975 at the age 103, although she insisted, only
weeks before her death, that she was merely 99.

On the trail,
STEPHEN BLY

For a list of other books by Stephen Bly
or information regarding speaking engagements
write:

Stephen Bly
Winchester, Idaho 83555